Total-E-Bound Publishing books by K.M. Mahoney:

Odd Man In
In Teddy's Arms

I0542494

THE LONELY HEART

K.M. MAHONEY

The Lonely Heart
ISBN # 978-1-78184-549-3
©Copyright K.M. Mahoney 2012
Cover Art by Oliver Bennett ©Copyright September 2012
Interior text design by Claire Siemaszkiewicz
Total-E-Bound Publishing

This is a work of fiction. All characters, places and events are from the author's imagination and should not be confused with fact. Any resemblance to persons, living or dead, events or places is purely coincidental.

All rights reserved. No part of this publication may be reproduced in any material form, whether by printing, photocopying, scanning or otherwise without the written permission of the publisher, Total-E-Bound Publishing.

Applications should be addressed in the first instance, in writing, to Total-E-Bound Publishing. Unauthorised or restricted acts in relation to this publication may result in civil proceedings and/or criminal prosecution.
The author and illustrator have asserted their respective rights under the Copyright Designs and Patents Acts 1988 (as amended) to be identified as the author of this book and illustrator of the artwork.

Published in 2012 by Total-E-Bound Publishing, Think Tank, Ruston Way, Lincoln, LN6 7FL, United Kingdom.

No part of this book may be reproduced, scanned, or distributed in any printed or electronic form without permission. Please do not participate in or encourage piracy of copyrighted materials in violation of the authors' rights. Purchase only authorised copies.

Total-E-Bound Publishing is an imprint of Total-E-Ntwined Limited.

If you purchased this book without a cover you should be aware that this book is stolen property. It was reported as "unsold and destroyed" to the publisher and neither the author nor the publisher has received any payment for this "stripped book".

THE LONELY HEART

Dedication

For anyone who's ever felt different. There is someone
out there for you.

Chapter One

Darn, irritating…

Isaiah flung his arm out, slapping blindly at the table. He gave a satisfied grunt upon finally finding the snooze button. He rolled over, folded the pillow around his head, and buried his nose into the mattress.

The buzzing continued. Isaiah groaned and pulled the pillow tighter around his ears. When that didn't work, he hit the button a few more times.

After several sluggish moments, realisation crept into his fuzzy brain. *Not the alarm clock.*

"Hellfire and damnation," he cursed. As usual, the sheets had inexplicably wrapped themselves around his legs. As he struggled to free himself, the blasted phone just kept ringing. He could ignore it, but…

Isaiah squinted at the glowing green numbers of his alarm clock. *Oh.* It wasn't that late after all. So, hopefully not an emergency.

Of course, now he was up.

Isaiah managed to escape from the sheets. He staggered across the room, cursing as his thighs protested. Stupid cow, and the mud hole, then the darn fence…

He dug through the pockets of his stiff, grime-encrusted jeans, crowing triumphantly when his fingers closed around the hard plastic case.

"'Lo?"

"Good evening. I'm trying to reach Isaiah Preston."

Well, hell. Either a sales call or bad news.

It ended up being bad news. Listening numbly, Isaiah would really have rather had someone trying to sell him a useless magazine subscription.

"Sorry," he said, interrupting the secretary mid-stream. "Could you repeat that?"

"Mr Sofina wanted to enquire as to when we could expect you. Elanore Preston's will was very specific, but there are still formalities that must be covered and permanent arrangements must be made."

"Elanore's dead?"

The woman stopped talking and Isaiah could hear the discomfort in the silence. "You weren't informed?"

"No." Isaiah knew he was being blunt to the point of rude, but really, couldn't she just get to the damn point? Elanore was his stepmother, not his mother. Hell, he'd only met the woman once, when she married his dad, and that was damn near ten years ago.

"You're next of kin."

Isaiah rolled his eyes. "That makes absolutely no sense," he said. "We weren't related and she and my father divorced two years ago." A mere six months before his father had died of a heart attack. He had been significantly older than his pretty little trophy wife.

"I'm afraid there's no one else. We can keep searching, but that will mean putting Josh in the foster care system."

"Josh?"

"Your brother."

Isaiah dropped the phone. It glanced off his foot and he howled a curse as it smacked a large bruise where Bunny had stepped on him earlier this week.

Only Tommy would name his half-draught monstrosity of a horse Bunny Rabbit. Maybe he should have got that x-ray, after all.

Isaiah scrambled to retrieve the phone, hoping the call hadn't been disconnected when the device had skittered across the hardwood floor. "Sorry. Could you repeat that? Brother? Since when do I have a brother?"

"Josh is, let's see…" The sound of rustling papers came over the line. "Ah. He's ten years old. Parents listed as Elanore and Harold Preston."

A half-brother. *Shit. Shit. Shit.*

Isaiah rubbed his forehead. "Ten. Christ. Okay, where do I need to be?"

He didn't even need to think about it. Blood was blood and Isaiah wasn't about to leave a kid hanging.

"San Francisco."

"Hang on." Isaiah rummaged up a pad and pencil and started scribbling notes. The woman spoke rapidly and by the time he finished writing, he had an aching hand and three pages covered in his smudged scrawl.

"I'll be there as soon as I can," Isaiah said. His head was swimming, thoughts spinning so quickly he couldn't quite grasp any one of them.

Josh. His little brother. His responsibility now. Christ. What was Isaiah going to do with a kid? He lived on a ranch in the middle of Wyoming. Josh would need a school and a house and...shit. Isaiah rubbed at his forehead again. Okay. One issue at a time. Pack a bag. Find a flight out to California. Talk to the lawyer. Work through the problems as they came along before he drowned.

Grady. Shit and damn. What was he going to tell Grady?

Isaiah dug through his dresser, tossing clothes into his battered duffle bag. He stifled a yawn as he zipped it closed. After yanking on his well-worn boots, Isaiah grabbed his jacket and his bag and jogged out to the truck. He tossed the duffle into the back and dragged his jacket on over his long-sleeved T-shirt. Only nine, but the night air was growing chillier by the day.

Now, he just had to talk to Grady. Isaiah turned up the sheepskin collar on his denim jacket and shoved his hands into the pockets, crossing the hard-packed ground with long strides. The lights on the corners of the barn shone dimly, casting large shadows across the yard. He hopped up the steps to the house, boots echoing loudly on the wood.

The porch was dark, the house still and quiet. Dang it all—he hated to wake up Grady. The ranch owner had worked nearly as hard as Isaiah to pull that idiot calf and his mama out of the mud puddle surrounding Wilson Pond. But he didn't have much choice. The boss deserved to know that his ranch manager was taking off for a few days.

Isaiah reluctantly rapped on the edge of the screen door, then stuffed his hand back in his pocket, hunched his shoulders, and waited. After a few minutes of silence, he knocked again.

The porch light flicked on, nearly blinding him, before the door creaked open.

"Isaiah? What the hell?"

"Sorry about the hour, Grady," he apologised. "But I got a call a few minutes ago and I needed to talk to you."

Serious brown eyes studied him before Grady nodded, holding the door open. "Sure, man. Come on in."

Isaiah stepped into the hall. "I've got a big favour to ask."

Grady waved his hand. "Ask away. But don't you want to sit down first?"

He shook his head. "I need to get going."

"Going?" Grady asked. "Where the hell are you going?"

"I'll be back," Isaiah hastened to assure his boss, seeing his distress. "But it seems my stepmom—well, former stepmom—was killed in a car accident a few days ago."

"Um, sorry?"

"Hell, I hardly knew the woman. But it seems she knew me, or at least of me, 'cause she named me her next of kin."

Surprise flickered across Grady's strong, weather-beaten face. "Huh."

"There's a kid."

"Oh, shit."

"Yeah. He's ten. This is the first I've heard, but he's family, you know? So I need a few days to get to California, figure out what to do."

"Done."

"I might...well, I'm not sure what to..." Isaiah stuttered, not really sure what he wanted to say.

"Bring him back with you. We'll manage."

Isaiah let out the breath he didn't know he'd been holding. "I really appreciate this."

Grady shook his head. "Just get out of here. The sooner you leave, the sooner I can get my manager back. Damned if I want to run this place by myself."

Isaiah grinned. "I'll hurry."

A few minutes later, Isaiah was firing up his truck and pulling onto the drive. He opened the window long enough to stick his arm out and wave at Grady. His boss stood on the porch under the dim glow of the outside light and waved back.

As the familiar sight dropped behind him, Isaiah sighed and slouched down into his seat, trying to get comfortable. It was going to be a long couple of days.

* * * *

Isaiah blinked rapidly, trying to push his exhaustion away. He was about ready to fall asleep standing up. The last few days had been endless.

He realised he was swaying and shook his head. Some of the fog cleared momentarily and he reached down, brushing wispy strands of pale hair off Josh's forehead. The kid was sound asleep, round face looking damn near cherubic.

Josh seemed so peaceful. And happy. The sight made Isaiah's gut churn. There was anger there and...well, a really healthy dose of guilt. Anger at the kid's mom for not telling Isaiah about Josh, about the problems, the whole guardianship thing—hell, for dying. Guilt for not finding out sooner, not digging, even though she wasn't family, not really.

Isaiah finally pulled himself away from his little brother, dropping down onto the other bed in the tiny hotel room he'd rented for the night. He scrubbed his face with one hand, squeezed his eyes closed and concentrated on breathing. All day, he'd had to put up a cheerful front, not wanting to upset Josh. Not wanting to disrupt the kid's excitement. But now, with Josh asleep, he could let go.

What Isaiah really wanted was a good stiff drink, but he figured that probably wasn't the best idea. He could turn on the television and try to distract himself — Josh was out so soundly it would take an explosion to wake him — but that didn't really appeal, either.

He wanted someone to talk to. Oh, hell, might as well be honest. He wanted someone to vent to. And only one name popped into his head.

Isaiah suppressed a growl, punching the buttons on his cell phone viciously. He leaned against the headboard, listening to the phone ring. A soft sound of frustration escaped, and he scrunched the pillows up behind his back, trying to ignore the way the ugly bedspread scratched against his bare legs.

"Grady."

The low, rough voice had an instant effect on Isaiah's fury. It was like a milkshake on a throat ablaze from spicy foods, soothing, coating him in a blanket of protection. Whenever things went wrong, Isaiah could always count on Grady to listen to the rant, sympathise, then plot. And right now, he needed reassurance in a way he hadn't before.

"Hey, man, how's it going?" Isaiah couldn't bring himself to cut straight to the problem. He could predict what Grady was going to say, but that didn't mean he wasn't nervous about broaching the subject. The whole damn situation was complicated and just plain wrong.

"Good," Grady replied, confusion clear in the deep tones. "Not that I'm not happy to hear from you, but—"

Isaiah cut him off with a heavy sigh which, even to him, sounded incredibly weary. "Yeah. Listen, I had no clue, huh? No one told me about Josh, and I certainly didn't know about all the rest. If I had…"

"You're not making a whole lot of sense," Grady pointed out. "Spit it out, already."

"I'm not sure bringing Josh back with me is the best idea," Isaiah said, rapidly enough that the words ran together. Damn it, even saying the words hurt. He wanted to be back home, with the horses and the cows and the boys and Grady. Especially with Grady.

"Wait, what? Isaiah, I need you! What the hell are you talking about, not coming back? Talk to me," Grady ordered. "What's going on?"

"It's Josh," Isaiah said. "I'm not sure the ranch is the best place for him. I swear, Grady, no one said anything."

"About what?"

"Josh can't speak."

A sharp intake greeted his announcement. Isaiah realised he was holding his breath, waiting for a reaction, and he forced his lungs to move again.

"I'm…sorry?" Grady's statement came out more like a question.

"What are you apologising for?" Isaiah asked.

"Dunno, just seemed like the thing to say."

"Yeah, well, I guess I'm sorry, too. There was an accident when Josh was little, severe damage to his vocal cords and throat. He was just starting to talk, too, so it was pretty devastating."

"Can't they, I don't know, fix that?"

"They tried. He had surgery when he was four, to put everything to rights. But that was, what, six years ago? And he still hasn't said a word. Apparently, he's been to doctors and psychiatrists and speech

14

pathologists. They threw out a lot of terms like selective mutism and developmental aphasia and were generally fucking worthless. According to the social worker, they talked about therapy and medications, but mostly thought it would just take time."

"But it didn't."

"No," Isaiah said, battling the urge to scream or cry or run away. Something. Anything.

"Look, we can handle it." There was a note in Grady's voice that Isaiah had never heard before. "It won't be easy, but come home, Isaiah."

Isaiah sighed again, this time with relief. After all, Grady was his boss. Who was Isaiah to ignore a direct order?

"All right," he finally agreed. "We've got a hotel near the airport for the night, but we'll head back tomorrow. I should be home in a day or so, depending on flights."

"Good. We need you here."

"Yeah. I think I need to be there, too."

They talked for a while longer, mostly ranch business, a little about the weather. Casual, easy conversation that helped Isaiah rid himself of the last of his anger. When he finally hung up, Isaiah was surprised to see that he'd been talking to Grady for nearly an hour.

Isaiah stood and stretched. Shower, bed, airport by six a.m. tomorrow. Maybe jack off in the shower, and if the face in his imagination looked a lot like Grady's, well, no one had to know. Then it was home and God, he couldn't wait.

Even if he had the nagging feeling that nothing was going to be the same when he got there.

Chapter Two

Isaiah pulled his truck to a dusty stop next to the massive barn, cutting the engine and grinning widely. Damn, but it was good to be home. And the Red Bar Ranch — long ago shortened to just the Branch — *was* home, no two ways about it. Over the years, the place had become as much his as Grady's, though the boss would probably argue with Isaiah on that.

The rambling farmhouse held court on one side of the yard, windows gleaming in the late autumn sun. It was a massive building, three stories tall if you counted the attic, which Isaiah did. There was a staircase, after all.

Grady put a lot of effort into keeping the place looking good, and it showed. Dark grey siding blended nicely with the oak trees surrounding the house. The trees were old, big and provided nice shade when the summer sun beat down.

The Grady family had been running cattle on this land for generations, each new owner adding their own touches. The yard now boasted one main barn with forty stalls and an indoor arena. Two smaller barns tucked off to one side held the breeding operation — right side horses, left side cattle. Fences stretched off into the distance, faint dark patches marring the vista, marking cattle or horses out to pasture. The majority of the herd was still farther out, closer to the mountains. Just a few short weeks now, and Grady would hire on some extra hands while they moved the herd. What they didn't sell off would be housed close enough to get to with the truck.

It was a solid operation, and Isaiah always felt a thrill of pride when he looked around.

A prickling at the back of his neck had Isaiah looking to his right. Josh stared at Isaiah, grinned, then looked through the window at the nearest corral, where two mares were munching contentedly near the fence. Isaiah chuckled.

"Go ahead," Isaiah said with a wave. "Just stay on this side of the fence. And be careful," he added to Josh's retreating figure. The kid had wasted no time leaping from the truck.

Isaiah followed, albeit with a lot less haste.

Grady stepped around the corner of the barn, ambling over with that loose-hipped stride of his, as Isaiah was retrieving their bags.

"Hey, boss," Isaiah called.

"You look like shit," Grady said bluntly.

"Gee, nice to see you too."

Grady scowled and Isaiah laughed.

"It was a long few days," Isaiah admitted, rubbing at the back of his neck.

"Glad you're back," Grady said. "Place started to fall apart. The guys don't get a damn thing done without you ridin' their asses."

"Thought that was your job," Isaiah returned.

Grady snorted.

"That the kid?" he asked.

"No, it's a midget I picked up at a rest stop." Isaiah blinked. God, he must be tired. "Sorry. Yeah, that's Josh."

Grady moved off purposefully. "Well, don't you think you ought to introduce us?" he yelled over his shoulder. "He's gonna be staying here for a while, after all."

Isaiah rolled his eyes, slung the bags over his shoulder and followed his boss. He called Josh's name and the kid turned, jumping off the fence where'd he'd perched himself on the lowest wooden slat.

"This is Grady," Isaiah said. "He's the boss around here."

Josh smiled up at the large man. The wind ruffled his already messy hair as his bright eyes crinkled with pleasure. Isaiah chuckled. No one could say they weren't related, that was certain. Josh looked just like he had at that age.

Grady's hard features softened as he looked down at the pint-sized human. "Welcome, Josh. We're real glad you could come and stay."

Josh blinked up at him and Grady received another one of those happy smiles.

Isaiah held out a bright red backpack. "Come on, kiddo," he said with a tired attempt at a smile of his own. "Let's get you settled and see about finding some food somewhere. You can come back and visit the horses later, promise."

Isaiah ended up talking to Josh's back, his brother drawn to the horses again. Isaiah shook his head and chuckled. That, too, was just like Isaiah at that age.

"The guys are scattered around," Grady said. "But I'm sure they'll come out of the woodwork to meet our newest resident. And if you need to get work done, you've got plenty of built-in babysitters. They'll watch out for him."

Isaiah chuckled. That was for damn sure. For all their tough exteriors, Grady's cowboys were big softies, particularly when it came to kids. Marshmallow centres, one and all.

Grady suddenly laughed, the sound one Isaiah hadn't heard in quite some time. "Heck, you might have problems keeping Tommy from adopting Josh."

Okay, now that was odd. All of a sudden, Grady seemed almost...cheerful? Damn, that was an unusual sight. Maybe having a kid around would be good for all of them.

Grady was nearly back at the house when he suddenly stopped and turned. "Oh. And bring Josh up to the house for dinners. No kid should be exposed to the crap you guys eat down there."

Isaiah couldn't do anything but stare, mouth open. Well, heck. What alien had snatched his boss and left someone...personable in his place? Surely Isaiah hadn't been gone *that* long.

Isaiah physically shook the thought from his head and grabbed his bag, leaving the mystery of Grady's sudden personality change for later, when he wasn't so tired. He stopped briefly to retrieve Josh, steering the small body towards the bunkhouse. He was quickly finding out that herding a kid was a lot harder than herding cattle. He finally ended up grabbing one small hand to keep Josh pinned to his side instead of darting after everything that caught his attention.

Whatever the locals said about Grady as a person — mainly certain adjectives like grumpy, irritable, quick-tempered and damned stubborn — he treated his employees well. The bunkhouse was a rambling, two-storey building, comfortable and solid, that sat a few hundred yards from the main house. The first floor took up more space than the second, which was mostly a combination of a games room and a hangout. Kept the boys from traipsing off to town all the time and kept the drinking to a minimum.

The front entrance opened into a large dining room. Off to one corner, forming an 'L', was the kitchen. It was comparably small next to the massive dining room, but considering most of the current gang's culinary skills consisted of burning things on a grill, it hadn't been a problem. A long hallway stretching to the back of the house led to a half-dozen rooms, almost like a college dorm setup, but nicer and with more privacy. Better bathrooms, too—three of them with oversized showers. The guys tended to drag a lot of dirt in with them.

Isaiah's room was towards the back, bigger than the others. Most of the rooms were doubles—two twin beds, a pair of desks, two large dressers, with a couple of corners left over for large, comfortable chairs and maybe a bookshelf. Isaiah's room, while the same size, was a single. Tucked into a corner of the big building where it was a bit quieter, he had a double bed, his own television setup and a couple of niceties not found in the other rooms, including a private bathroom. Isaiah still wasn't sure what he was going to do long-term, but for now, he'd decided to crash in one of the empty dormers with his little brother.

It wasn't that Isaiah thought anything would happen. He guessed he was just being a paranoid control freak. He should probably look into getting a place in town for the two of them. Not ideal—it would mean a good half-hour drive twice a day. He just didn't see many other options.

Isaiah let Josh go into the room first. Josh turned his head back and forth, blond hair flopping and eyes wide as he spun in a circle. He looked back at Isaiah, bright green eyes still gleaming with excitement. Josh had, from all accounts, led a pretty sheltered life, so this must be quite the adventure for him.

"I guess we're gonna go join Grady for dinner later, but we should have enough time for a tour."

Isaiah wasn't stupid enough to turn down an invitation for a dinner away from the bunkhouse. It was Tuesday, which meant Joseph's turn to cook, an event to be avoided at all costs. The mere thought made his stomach churn with nausea. Joseph was darn near famous throughout the county. Or infamous, rather. He'd been known to ruin takeout.

Josh dropped onto one of the beds, bouncing a few times. He looked so happy that Isaiah had to smile. He sat down next to his brother and draped his arm over the skinny shoulders.

"I take it you like it here, huh?"

Josh gave him a quick hug, still bouncing. Isaiah made a mental note to keep a close eye on the kid's sugar intake.

Isaiah sighed, thinking of the million and two things he still had to do today. When he jerked himself back to the present, it was to find Josh looking up at him expectantly. Isaiah laughed, able to read his brother's thoughts as easily as if he had spoken them.

"I haven't forgotten. I'll talk to Grady tonight about getting you up on a horse. Don't worry, we'll keep you plenty busy."

Fresh air and lots of outdoor activities. It would be good for Josh. His brother was a little on the pale and scrawny side. Not unhealthy, just...a city kid. But that was okay. If Isaiah knew anything about his guys, they'd make a proper little cowboy out of Josh within two weeks. Probably less.

Isaiah stood up, grabbing Josh under the arms and swinging him around. Josh giggled as Isaiah set him on his feet.

"How about a quick tour?" Isaiah asked. "I can check up on the guys and you can get a proper introduction to all the horses."

Isaiah had to move quickly to keep up with the kid. He sighed again, wondering how the hell he was going to come up with enough energy to ride herd on the rascal. Isaiah may not have spent much time around kids, but it seemed like Josh had enough energy for three people his size.

Isaiah caught up with Josh at the barn, grabbing Josh's waist and swinging him up into the air again.

"Hold on, kiddo," he scolded mildly. "We've got some rules to lay down. First off, stay out of the stalls. Second, horses spook easily. So move slowly and keep the noise to a minimum."

At that last bit, Josh gave Isaiah a disgusted look. Isaiah cracked up at the expression, laughing so hard he had to hold his sides.

"Right," he said when he could breathe again. "No problem there. On to rule number three, then. Don't go wandering too far without someone around. It's easy to get lost out here. Rule four—"

"Keep talking and the kid's not gonna remember a word you said."

Isaiah rolled his eyes. "Don't you have a fence to mend somewhere, Tommy?"

Tommy clucked his tongue. "Touchy today, aren't we?"

Isaiah glared, but there wasn't much force behind it. "Josh, this is Tommy. Tommy—my little brother."

Tommy bent over and shook Josh's hand. "Nice to meet you," he said with a serious face. Josh returned the look. Then they both burst into giggles. Isaiah thought to himself that a man of Tommy's size really shouldn't giggle. It was kind of disturbing.

Tommy Henderson was their newest hand, an ex-bull rider Grady had picked up about a year ago. Isaiah had nearly swallowed his tongue in shock when Grady had shown up with Tommy in tow after a buying trip. Seemed Tommy had taken a bad spill and had decided that perhaps riding crazy twisters of death—complete with horns—wasn't the best career option. Grady had offered him a job on the spot, for reasons only the boss understood.

Tommy had arrived, six-foot-six of bruised and tattered muscle. Heck, they'd had to go out and buy him a horse as none of their current stock could carry the man's bulk. They'd ended up with a gelding that looked like it had more than a little Clydesdale in it and was butt-ugly, to boot. The oh-so-famous Bunny Rabbit, whose massive hooves had left bruises on everyone on the ranch. Tommy loved the stupid thing, though, and couldn't have doted on it more if it was his child.

Since then, Isaiah had learnt that Tommy had a skewed sense of humour and a sharp tongue. But he was one heck of a roper and a hard worker, so Isaiah put up with it. And, on the rare occasion, enjoyed the hell out of it.

Tommy straightened. "Thought Joey was going to start doing handstands when he heard you were back. He hates being in charge."

"I know. Where is he?"

"Back thirty," Tommy said, pointing over his shoulder. "You might want to go rescue Micah. Joey has him re-stringing the gulch."

Isaiah groaned and pinched his nose between his thumb and forefinger. "I'm gonna smack that boy. All right. Josh, you want to hang out with Tommy a while? I have to go rescue Micah."

Joseph—Joey only to Tommy, who thought their names should match for some unknown reason—was a good man and a top-notch hand. He just got a little enthusiastic sometimes. Isaiah left him in charge because he trusted Joseph to fetch Grady if things got out of hand, rather than sweeping it aside until Isaiah could return. But neither of them really liked the situation. Joseph wasn't cut out to be a leader and he was honest enough to admit it.

Tommy grinned and clapped Josh on the shoulder. He had to bend a bit to do it, with the huge height difference. "We'll get along just fine, FL. Come on, buddy, let me introduce you to Bunny."

Tommy led an eager Josh off to meet the elephant masquerading as a horse in their barn. Isaiah shook his head in exasperation, though the emotion was tinged with fondness. Tommy was unique, for sure. He'd started calling Isaiah 'FL' his first day on the job—it stood for Fearless Leader, from Tommy's favourite cartoon.

* * * *

Isaiah fetched his horse, Tobias, from a nearby corral and saddled up the dusty brown gelding. He took off to the west at a slow lope, eager to get back to work.

It took him ten minutes to cut across the pasture. He heard his employees long before he saw them.

"Hold it tighter, would you?"

"I'm trying. Stop pushing me, dammit."

"Would you stop being such a wuss?"

"So help me God, Joseph, I'm gonna smack you with this fence post if you don't shut up!"

Isaiah reined to a stop and sat for a minute, leaning his hands on the saddle horn and watching his bickering cowhands. Micah gripped one end of the barbed wire, feet braced against the base of a thick piece of wood, while Joseph guided the wire. They were trying to wrap and secure the beginning of this section, preparing to stretch the fencing across the narrow strip of bare ground between the nearest pasture and the gulch—more of a gully, really—that ran alongside said pasture. Cattle had a tendency to fall into the wide trench, so they'd fence it, then a hard rain would come and erosion would wash away the fence. Then they'd string it again.

The current attempt wasn't going well. Micah and Joseph were cussing up a storm and kept tripping over each other's feet.

"I leave ya'll alone for a couple of days and the whole place goes to shit," Isaiah drawled.

"Boss!"

Joseph looked over in relief and dropped his hammer. Right on Micah's foot. Micah dropped the rolled section of wire, howling. Isaiah rolled his eyes. With the shit-kickers Micah was wearing, the damn idiot would have hardly felt a thing.

Clearly thinking the same thing, Joseph yanked off his hat and smacked Micah in the shoulder with it. Damn, his crew was turning into a regular comedy troop. Isaiah blamed Tommy—he was obviously rubbing off on the others.

"Glad you're back, boss." Joseph cleared his throat and donned his hat again, trying to regain some composure.

"Agreed," Micah seconded wholeheartedly.

Isaiah grinned at the abashed pair, looking like nothing so much as a pair of boys caught trying to sneak out of their bedroom after midnight.

"Listen, boss—"

He held his hand up, not really wanting to hear any convoluted explanations. Joseph clamped his mouth shut.

Joseph had been at the Branch nearly as long as Isaiah. He'd been hired as a stable hand at seventeen, mucking out stalls and exercising horses. He'd been the first one to start calling Isaiah 'boss'. Said it just didn't feel right calling the ranch foreman by his name. For some reason, though, he had no problem calling Grady by his name. So Isaiah called Grady 'boss,' the hands called Isaiah 'boss' and Grady 'Grady' and, despite seeming confusing as hell at first glance, it all worked out.

He swung down out of the saddle and dropped the reins to the ground. Tobias immediately started grazing.

Isaiah settled his hat more firmly on his head. "All right, boys. Let's get to work."

He yanked on his gloves and waded in.

God, he loved this place.

Chapter Three

Isaiah hesitated at the front door, a little uncertain of protocol. Aw, hell. Since when did he —

Josh barrelled right past him. The screen door banged shut in Isaiah's surprised face before he could catch the little pipsqueak.

He yelled Josh's name but really, what could he do? He followed the kid into the warm, welcoming interior of Grady's house. Seeing no sign of Josh, Isaiah shook his head philosophically. Grady would have to get used to Josh sooner or later. *Might do the man some good to get his neat little world shaken up a bit.*

Isaiah shrugged off his coat, hanging both it and his hat on the pegs near the door. Shoving his hands into his front pockets, he wandered through the living room, around the corner and down the short hall into Grady's spacious kitchen.

Josh was already there, perched on a chair, feet swinging above the floor.

Grady stood at the counter, busy chopping a tomato. He greeted Isaiah without turning.

"I see the munchkin found you," Isaiah said.

"That he did. Take a seat, I'm just about ready."

"It smells good." Isaiah sat next to Josh, feeling strangely awkward. And why that would be, he had no idea. He'd known Grady for going on eight years. They spent more time together in a normal day than most married couples.

This felt different, though.

Isaiah sat in slightly uncomfortable silence, tapping his fingers on the table until Josh glared at him.

"Want to get the salad out of the fridge for me, Josh?" Grady asked.

Josh hurried across the room, coming back with a bowl nearly as big as he was. Isaiah reached out to rescue it before the whole thing tilted to the floor.

Grady already had a covered pan on the table and he joined them a minute later with a plate of bread and another of sliced vegetables. He shrugged at Isaiah's questioning look.

"Figured the kid might not like some of this junk on his salad."

Isaiah shook his head and proceeded to follow Grady's lead, dishing himself generous portions and dumping all kinds of 'junk' on his own pile of lettuce, the smell almost making Isaiah drool in anticipation.

For a tiny thing, Josh could put away an astonishing amount of food. Isaiah paused to watch in amazement when his little brother dished up his fourth helping of spaghetti. Grady cocked his head and looked across the table.

"Guess we'll need more food next time," he said.

"No kidding. When you said I could bring Josh here, I'm sure you didn't expect him to eat you into bankruptcy."

Josh looked up from his meal with a scowl. He stuck his tongue out and went right back to munching on the crisp edges of his sixth piece of garlic bread.

Grady chuckled, a low and rich sound that was rare enough it made Isaiah's own lips curl up into a half-smile. It also made his pants a little tight, but he had become used to the sensation enough to ignore it.

"We got that fence line strung up around the gully."

"Again?" Grady asked. "Hell, why do you even bother anymore? First good rain's just gonna take it out."

"Gives the boys something to do, I guess."

Grady snorted. "The boys have enough to do."

"Maybe I just want to keep them out of trouble for a bit."

"Now that I believe."

Silence fell for a minute while Isaiah slurped up some more spaghetti. "Joseph handled things pretty well in my absence."

"Yeah, just don't do it too often. Never seen a body so stressed. Thought he was gonna give himself a heart attack a couple of times. Tommy didn't help."

"No, he wouldn't. What's on the agenda for tomorrow? Anything I need to catch up on?"

Grady shook his head. "We're doing okay. But I want to start moving the outer herds closer this week, get them ready to ship."

Isaiah nodded. "I'll probably send Micah and Tommy out to take care of that, then. We've got a couple of late calves in the Wilson pasture. I thought I might check on them in the morning."

Josh, who had been following the conversation with half an ear, kicked Isaiah under the table.

"Brat," Isaiah scolded fondly. He looked over at Grady. Dark hazel eyes studied them impassively.

Isaiah wished, yet again, that his boss was easier to read. "I was wondering if you might have time to give Josh some riding lessons."

"Course I do. Can't have someone on a ranch who can't ride. That's just wrong."

"Yep."

Josh bounced in his seat. Grady chuckled again and passed over a napkin. "You look like a vampire," he told Josh.

Isaiah let out a burst of startled laughter. Josh wiped his mouth. Spaghetti sauce still clung to his cheeks, clear up to his nose. Isaiah grabbed another napkin and finished the job. Josh squirmed under the ministrations.

"If you're done, you can go watch some TV in the main room," Grady told him. "Your big brother can help me with the dishes."

Josh made a hasty escape with the speed only attained by a kid avoiding chores.

"He could have helped," Isaiah pointed out.

"Time enough for that later," Grady replied easily. "Let him enjoy his first day before we start putting him to work."

Grady watched Isaiah from the corner of his eye. The tall, lean cowboy moved with unconscious grace as he cleared the table. Grady turned the water on in the sink and added soap, careful not to get caught staring.

It had been a long time since he'd enjoyed a meal that much. Having Isaiah and Josh at the table had almost made him feel like part of a family again.

"Josh is a great kid," he said awkwardly. The silence was growing and, while Isaiah seemed completely at ease, it was making Grady nervous.

"Yeah, he is." Isaiah's lips turned up in that charming half-smile that Grady loved so much. "Smart and stubborn. He's gonna grow up to be quite a man."

"How's he handling his mom's death?" Grady asked, scrubbing at the sauce stains on a plate.

"Surprisingly well, but I get the feeling they weren't very close. Josh has spent most of his life at some boarding school."

"Wasn't he a bit young?" Grady couldn't imagine a mom, any mom, sending a toddler away like that.

Isaiah shrugged, eyes dark with some nameless emotion. "I think so, but I gather it was a special school for kids with disabilities. Guess she thought it was best for him."

"Still doesn't seem quite right."

Silence fell over the kitchen, both of them feeling awkward now. Grady searched for another topic, but his brain seemed to have stuttered to a halt. He handed a plate to Isaiah. Their fingers met, tangled for a second, and it was all Grady could do to keep from groaning even at that brief touch. Damn, he was pathetic. Grady looked away before Isaiah could see and identify the longing in his eyes.

He cleared his throat. "So, riding lessons," he said, grasping at the first idea that sprang into his head.

Isaiah grinned. "Yeah. Josh has his heart set on learning to ride."

"You don't want to teach him?" Grady asked curiously. He would have thought it would be something Isaiah wanted to do—pass on that kind of knowledge to his little brother.

"There's plenty I can teach him besides riding a horse. I figure since you usually stick pretty close to the main barns during the day anyway, it would give you two a chance to get to know one another. After all, he's ours...here. You know."

Isaiah's cheeks flushed red as he stumbled over his words. Grady felt a deep sense of pleasure spread through him before he shook it off. Isaiah hadn't meant it that way, of course. Just a little conversational blip.

"I'll look forward to it," Grady said. Damn, he had hoped that wouldn't sound as awkward and formal out loud as it did in his head.

Isaiah gave him another strange look, the same one he'd been turning on Grady all evening. They finished the rest of the clean-up in silence. Isaiah gathered Josh soon after and they said their good nights.

Grady closed the door and stood there for a minute. He dropped his head forward, thumping it on the wood.

"Stupid," he cursed himself in a soft voice. "So stupid." He couldn't have thought of something to talk about, something to do, to prolong the evening? No, of course not. Probably just as well, since apparently he was an anti-social idiot who couldn't figure out how to hold a decent conversation.

Grady locked up the house and flicked off the lights before trudging upstairs. He fell face-first onto his bed with a groan. He rolled onto his back and grabbed a pillow, yelling into it in pure frustration. For eight endless years he'd watched Isaiah with respect, then admiration, then a confusing turmoil of feelings that had sorted themselves out into something ridiculously like a teenage crush. And just like a teenager, at the first real social opportunity he'd got with the man who starred in most of his dreams, he'd choked.

Grady shoved the pillow aside and climbed off the bed. Maybe jacking off in the shower would help him sleep. It had become a regular part of his routine lately. A depressing one, in some ways because, as usual, he would picture Isaiah there with him. And, as usual, it was all in his imagination. And very unlikely to ever turn into reality. After all, Grady had been given plenty of time to make his move. If he hadn't mustered the courage yet, he might as well accept that he never would.

Grady turned the water on full-blast, cranking the knob to damned-near scalding. He stripped, chucking the clothes in the general vicinity of the hamper. He didn't bother checking to see if he'd hit or missed.

Thick steam enveloped him as he stepped into the shower. He braced his hands on the still chilly tiles, leaning his head forward and letting the water batter at his shoulders and back. He grimaced at the slight prickles of pain, the force of the water pounding away at the knots of tension in his muscles.

When the water went from searing to pleasant, he reached for the soap. The washcloth was scratchy against his skin, pebbling his nipples and sending little ripples along his abdomen. He kept moving lower, wanting, needing, yet reluctant. But, as always, he gave in.

He wrapped the soapy cloth around his cock, keeping the pressure light and steady. Steam billowed around him, encasing his private world, letting him hide away from reality.

In his imagination, he wasn't alone in the small shower. Strong arms closed around his waist, the warm body a solid presence behind him. A chin dropped onto his shoulder and that familiar, beloved voice whispered low encouragements in his ear.

"*Let me see,*" the Isaiah in Grady's imagination ordered gently. "*Show me how much you want me. I want to see you, see that thick cock harden. See you lose yourself in pleasure as you shoot your spunk all over the wall. Show me, Grady."*

Grady closed his eyes, obeying the voice of his imagined lover. He moaned, the sound low and quiet, almost lost beneath the pounding spray. His shaft was hard and aching under his touch. He dropped the washcloth as the slightly rough texture became too much. Nearly painful. He rubbed over the head of his cock and up the shaft, the skin hot and sensitive. As his hand moved, picking up speed, the calluses on his fingers caught against the delicate skin. The gentle drag sent shivers up his spine and made his balls draw up tight.

"Show me."

Grady could almost hear the words in the water's thrumming. He tugged one more time, the motion and the imagined words sending him hurtling towards release. Grady bit back a yell, the sensations making his knees go weak. Thick streams of spunk shot over his hand, coating his fingers, the wall, and even his feet when his grip faltered.

Grady breathed through his orgasm, blinking with unseeing eyes at the cracked blue tile around the faucet until his mind started working again.

He sighed, staring at his hand. He lifted it up, watching the water wash all signs of his orgasm away. The brief aura of contentment inspired by his fantasy was washed away just as easily. Grady could almost see it swirling down the drain.

"Goddamn it." He twisted the faucet off with a sharp motion. The hot water was about gone, anyway.

And he was a shitty liar, especially to himself.

Grady got out, cursing softly as his feet slipped on the ceramic tile. He snagged a towel and dried off with brisk, efficient motions. He wanted out of the bathroom. Now. Away from the scene of the crime, so to speak.

He let the now damp towel drop to the floor and wandered into the connecting bedroom. With another muttered epithet, he flopped facedown onto the bed.

"Grady," he told the dark blue fabric, "you're an absolute idiot."

Chapter Four

The weather was crisp and clear, the sound of horses and cattle amplified in the still morning air. It was pleasant outside, no other people to disturb Grady's contemplation. Although he had to admit, maybe he should have grabbed a jacket to go over his sweatshirt. Each day grew a little colder and the clouds a touch heavier, reminding everyone that winter was on its way.

Grady braced his shoulder against the raw wood post, cradling his third mug of coffee in his hands. Okay, so it was only six in the morning and he was already on caffeine overload. Sleep had been a little hard to come by lately. Nothing new there.

He sipped his coffee, again savouring the quiet from the shelter of his front porch. The ranch was just beginning to stir, the boys rolling out of their bunks with moans, groans and curses. The horses were shifting with the onset of restlessness, eager for their morning feed.

The bunkhouse door slammed and a small figure darted down the stairs. Grady's lips twitched as he watched the kid bounce across the yard. No caffeine needed for that one. What Grady wouldn't do for just a third of that energy.

Isaiah came barrelling out of the door on his brother's heels, yelling for Josh. The little squirt put on a burst of speed, sneakers smacking the ground rhythmically.

Isaiah caught him halfway across the yard, swooping down and wrapping his arms around Josh's waist. Isaiah scooped Josh up and mock-tackled him to the accompaniment of childish squeals and laughter.

Damn, but that was a nice sound. Grady's lips tilted up as he watched the brothers' antics. Isaiah had Josh tucked against his bigger frame, tickling and teasing. Josh was squirming and trying to break free, giggles ringing out the whole while.

They finished crossing the clearing that separated the bunkhouse from the main house. Isaiah kept Josh tucked against his side and Grady was struck again by how much the two brothers looked alike. Josh might be small now, but Grady could see the promise of sinewy strength and above-average height. The pair shared the same dark blond hair, with its tendency to stick up at the back. Their straight noses were a touch too large for their lean faces and their chins were slightly pointed.

And they both had the same smile, wide lips bracketed by deep creases in Isaiah's case, the remainder of baby fat in Josh's. Their smiles shone in their eyes, one pair of brown and one pair of green, and softened what could otherwise be stern, overly-sharp features. Once Josh hit the teenage years, they were going to look damn near like twins.

Grady really wanted to jog out to meet them. He longed to get swallowed up in the camaraderie and caring. His throat tightened with rising affection for each of them. He took a deep breath, hiding his expression behind his mug, and reminded himself again that Josh wasn't his to keep. And neither, as much as he wanted it, was Isaiah.

"Hey, boss. Gonna share?"

Grady looked up. Isaiah stared at Grady's mug with ill-concealed covetousness.

"I put on another pot before I came out," he said, pushing away from the post he'd been leaning against. "Should be about ready."

"I can't wait that long."

Isaiah reached over and tugged the mug from Grady's unresisting hands. Hell, he was too surprised to protest. Isaiah took a deep swallow, moaning in a way that went straight to Grady's cock. Luckily, Josh was watching his brother and not the suffering ranch owner. Grady shifted a bit, concealing the bulge in his jeans with the ease of long-standing practice.

Josh tapped Isaiah's leg and made a face. Isaiah laughed.

"It's an adult thing, I guess," Isaiah told Josh with a shrug. "We'll get you some milk or juice inside."

Josh didn't wait for an invitation. He bounced past Grady, tromping footsteps echoing through the house.

Grady took his mug back from Isaiah. There was something incredibly intimate about standing there in the still, chilly morning air sharing a cup of coffee.

"We should probably get inside and make sure the kid doesn't try to raid the cookie jar for breakfast," Isaiah said in a low voice. Was it just Grady's imagination, or were Isaiah's eyes focused on Grady's mouth?

Grady concluded a few seconds later that it must have been wishful thinking. Isaiah followed Josh inside without a backwards glance. Grady tossed the dregs from his cup into the nearest bush. Suddenly, a lot of the promise seemed to drain out of the morning. He squared his shoulders and took a deep breath.

He was doing that a lot lately. If he kept up the deep-breathing habit, he was gonna hyperventilate or something.

The brothers were in the kitchen already. Isaiah had made straight for the coffee pot. He must have moved with Superman's speed because he already had a cup in his hand and was busy trying to drain it in record time. Josh, for all his pent-up energy, moved a little slower. He was still pouring milk into his cereal bowl.

Grady's lips twitched, some of his bad mood leaching away—Josh had found his secret addiction. That was just like a kid. The Fruity Pebbles box sat open on the counter, removed from its hiding spot in the back of the pantry behind the Wheaties. Not that Grady ever ate the Wheaties. They were there for show, to cover up the kid's cereal box.

"Put the milk away," Grady reminded Josh. Josh paused, spoon halfway to his mouth and dripping milk off the sides like a white waterfall. He dropped the spoon back into the bowl with a little splash and obeyed before he climbed up on the chair, short legs swinging, and went back to eating with admirable focus.

Grady joined Isaiah at the counter, refilling his own cup. Dang, looked like he was going to need to make another pot. Isaiah had already damn near emptied this one. And in less than five minutes, too. It was impressive.

"You boys must have an industrial-size coffeemaker over there," Grady teased gently. "Otherwise you'd wear the thing out in less than a week."

Isaiah froze, lips plastered to the rim of his cup. He shrugged sheepishly. "We do have one of those twelve-cup ones," he admitted.

Grady laughed. "I don't even want to know how much you spend each month in coffee grounds."

"No, you don't." Isaiah's smile was…well, there was no other word for it but adorable. Chagrined and happy at the same time, it made him look young and carefree. Grady had to clench his free hand into a fist to keep from reaching for his foreman.

Piercing green eyes watched them from across the room. Josh was studying them intently. Or rather, he was studying Grady. There was a look on his face that made Grady want to squirm. Josh might be a kid, but he was very, very bright. There was a knowledge in his eyes that Grady didn't even want to attempt to decipher. Mostly because it would probably make him uncomfortable. Or embarrassed. It was too early for that.

Low voices filtered through the window as Micah and Tommy rounded the house on their way to the back stable. The two main breeding stables were near the bunkhouse, but when Grady had gone to expand, shortly after Isaiah took over as his foreman and business-slash-ranch manager, they'd been out of room over there. Fitting another barn in would have been impossible, unless they had chopped down a couple of dozen trees. Grady hadn't been willing to do that, not when there was a perfectly decent clearing on the back side of his house. The stable there now housed a large indoor training arena and all the mounts reserved for everyday use. It made for a bit of a walk for the boys, but no one seemed to mind.

The sounds of activity seemed to jolt Isaiah out of his caffeine haze. He put his cup down—after draining it, of course. That was one man who wouldn't dream of wasting a drop of coffee.

"I guess I'd better get out there. I want to check the southern pastures today, make sure the fence is solid for when we roust the cattle out of the foothills. Winter's gonna come fast this year, I'm thinking."

Grady nodded reluctantly. "Yeah. If you need me to help, holler. Oh, and I want to sit down and go over some business stuff with you later. Got a couple of invoices that have me tied up in knots. Maybe after dinner tonight?"

Isaiah nodded. "Sure thing, boss."

Isaiah turned his back to Grady, thankfully missing Grady's slight wince at the title. He paused briefly to ruffle his little brother's already messy hair.

"Be good for Grady," Isaiah admonished gently. "If you need anything I'll be around."

"We'll be fine," Grady assured Isaiah. "I'll call you around lunch time, bring something out to you guys. No sense hauling your asses all the way back."

"That would be great." Isaiah ruffled Josh's hair again and said his goodbyes, his long legs quickly taking him out of sight.

Josh put his spoon down next to his empty bowl, folded his hands on the table, and looked expectantly at Grady. Grady laughed and stuck his cup in the sink.

"All right, kid. Rinse out your bowl and we'll go see about getting you up on a horse."

They left the house a few minutes later, Josh holding onto Grady's hand while they walked across the yard.

Pint-sized legs had to make three steps to every one of Grady's, even though Grady was walking slower than usual. He smiled down at the tyke, feeling a rush of affection welling up. He might not have known the kid long, but Josh was already worming his way into Grady's heart. Part of that, Grady knew, was Josh's connection to Isaiah. He'd already turned most of his heart over to Isaiah—it wasn't hard to extend that to the little mini-Isaiah at his side.

But a lot of the growing affection was all for Josh. A cute, stubborn, energetic little kid who looked at life with an excitement that Grady envied. Most of the time, Josh didn't even seem to think about the fact that, according to the rest of the world, he was 'disabled'. Like Isaiah, Grady was determined to do everything in his power to keep Josh thinking that way.

Grady called out greetings to his men as they walked into the dim interior of the stable. Micah and Tommy looked up from where they were tightening girths and gave him nods of welcome and a low greeting in Micah's case. Tommy stayed quiet, but Grady didn't take offence. It took the large man a good two hours after waking for his brain to start working. Although, according to Joseph, Tommy's brain never started working and the sleepies had absolutely nothing to do with it.

Grady had spent the last year trying to figure out if the guys should just kiss and get over it, or if they simply fought like brothers, all argument and little heat. He was never very good at picking up on those kinds of non-verbal signals.

Isaiah and Joseph weren't in sight, but Grady hadn't expected them to be. Their first job of the day usually involved checking on the broodmares in the breeding stables on the other side of the bunkhouse. Cameras were set up in there, the pregnant mares watched closely, but Isaiah still liked the hands-on approach — he always preferred to check out the mares himself, pregnant or not. The first job of the day was making sure the girls close to delivery were comfortable before letting the mares out into their small paddocks to get some fresh air. There were usually treats involved somewhere, too. They bought carrots in the jumbo-sized bags at least twice a month.

Grady headed for the back of the stable and grabbed a halter off the wall next to one of the stalls.

"First lesson," he told Josh. Big green eyes looked up at him, Josh's face a study in concentration as he absorbed every word. It was nice, having such an attentive student.

Grady slipped the bolt on the sliding door and shoved it aside. "Always enter carefully. Jackson here is a gentle guy, but horses don't act rationally when they're startled."

He showed Josh how to slip the halter on and let the boy lead the horse from the stall and over to a nearby set of cross-ties. Dang, but that was a sight made for a picture. The little boy in his hoodie and sneakers, leading a horse six times his size, the rising sun lighting them with a soft glow through the barn doors.

Grady quickly found out Josh was a natural when it came to horses. Despite the way he usually bounced around, Josh possessed a calm manner and a soft touch that Jackson ate up. Grady watched the horse nudge Josh gently on the shoulder, earning a delighted laugh. Big brown eyes watched the boy as he picked up the reins and Grady had a feeling Jackson was a goner. The horse would probably follow Josh anywhere.

Grady finally called a halt to the riding lesson after about an hour and a half—he didn't want Josh to be too sore tomorrow. Josh had a natural feel for the horse and a good seat in the saddle. He didn't push or force but guided. Yep, the kid had the makings of a top-notch horseman.

"You did good, kid," Grady said quietly when Josh stopped in front of him. That cute face just beamed. Josh kept one hand wrapped tightly around the reins, the other resting on the gelding's shoulder. "Pretty soon you'll be taking off with the others."

Josh smiled, conveying his silent thanks. Grady smiled back.

"You're welcome." He ruffled Josh's hair, like Isaiah unable to resist the soft, unruly strands. The kid looked younger than his years, staring up at Grady with adoring eyes and just soaking up the praise, as if he wasn't used to hearing encouraging words. The thought made Grady sad.

"What do you say we put Jackson up and take some lunch out to Isaiah, hmm? We'll take the Jeep for today, but maybe tomorrow we can ride it out to them."

The words earned Grady another one of those happy smiles. Grady briefly clasped one skinny shoulder in his hand and squeezed before following Josh and his new best friend inside.

Chapter Five

"Looks okay." Grady used his boot to hold down one strand of barbed wire as he ducked under the second. He paused on the other side, looking back at the heifer grazing with bovine contentment. She'd been wobbling a bit when he and Josh first saw her, but after a quick inspection, seemed to be in one piece. He'd mention it to Isaiah, just to keep a watch. She was destined for his breeding programme and as it wasn't a large programme, he needed every gal he had.

Grady bent over and snatched up the reins off the ground. He tugged his gelding's head up. The action got him a baleful glare, soggy grass hanging out of the horse's mouth.

"Silly beast," Grady scolded. He slapped the side of Dixon's neck before swinging into the saddle.

"Ready?" Grady looked over at his travelling companion with a grin. Josh returned the expression. He waved his hand in a shooing motion and Grady laughed. "What, we on a time schedule I don't know about?"

Josh smirked and prodded Jackson into a slow jog.

Out of pure habit, Grady kept one eye on Josh, watching as the budding rider guided his horse around a puddle. Josh really didn't need any supervision—he sat in the saddle like he'd been born there, happy and relaxed, taking in everything around them with wide-eyed wonder.

They left the scattered herd of cattle behind, passing through a small stand of trees before cresting a small rise. Josh waved madly as several distant figures came into view. A tall shadow waved back equally madly, whole body getting into the motion. Grady couldn't stop a burst of laughter at Tommy's antics.

Josh and Grady had fallen easily into the habit of trekking out every day, lunch in tow. With winter rapidly approaching, the boys were spending most of the day on the range, rounding up the cows and pushing them closer, readying the majority of them to be loaded and hauled off for sale. Grady and Josh usually saddled up around ten or eleven, depending on how far they had to go, saddlebags heavy with sandwiches, chips and cookies. Lots of sandwiches, chips, and cookies. The boys always worked up impressive appetites. Tommy alone could put away a half-dozen sandwiches and still have room for more. The man was a bottomless pit. If Grady had known how much the former bull rider ate before he hired the man, he might have thought twice about his offer.

Micah greeted them with a bright smile. Tommy smacked the man on the back of the head as he headed straight for the food, ignoring the loud protest that followed.

"What'd you bring us today, squirt?" he asked Josh. The big man waggled his eyebrows, leering comically at the bags secured to the back of the boy's saddle. Josh laughed and shook his head, waving a finger.

"Patience isn't really Tommy's strong point," Micah drawled.

"No kidding," Grady replied dryly. "I would never have guessed."

His comment earned a sharp look from Micah. His hands had all been giving him similar looks lately. It was damned odd.

Tommy reached up and swung Josh off Jackson, bouncing him in the air a couple of times before setting him on his small feet. The kid looked like a real cowboy now, decked out in heavy jeans and miniature dark brown boots, with an adorable little cowboy hat covering his wild hair. Isaiah and Grady had taken him shopping his second day on the ranch. It had been a blast, picking out clothes for their budding ranch hand. Something about those little boots and hats…

It made Grady long for his own miniature cow hand. Not that such a thing was likely, but it didn't keep a guy from wishing.

"Where's Isaiah?" he asked, dismounting and unlatching the saddle bags secured to Dixon. He swung the heavy leather satchels off and slung them over his shoulder. Nearby, Micah was doing the same with the bags on Jackson.

"He and Joseph are clearing out the gully a couple miles west. They should be back soon."

"We don't have to wait for them, do we?" Tommy asked, hands already reaching out greedily. Micah moved out of range, smacking the back of Tommy's hand when it got too close.

K.M. Mahoney

Josh shook his head, rolling his eyes. He smirked at Tommy, making a little motion with his hand.

The three of them burst out laughing. Isaiah had been right, that first day. The kid could be so darn expressive that, more than once, Grady had forgotten he couldn't talk to them.

"I'm not that bad," Tommy protested. But he was grinning widely as he said it. "Most of the time," he added.

This time it was Micah's turn to roll his eyes. "So you weren't the reason Joseph put that padlock on the kitchen door?" he asked.

Tommy scowled. "Darned cowboy. I got him good for that one, if you'll remember."

"Now this is a story I haven't heard," Grady said.

Micah and Tommy had brought the truck out today. Tommy pulled some blankets out of the cab and they spread them out, settling down in the bed of the pickup to eat their lunch. Sitting on the ground now left a man with a distinct chill in his butt. It wouldn't be long before the boys would start staying closer to the main ranch and eating their lunches at the bunkhouse.

Micah laughed, handing Josh a roast beef sandwich wrapped in cling film. "You haven't? Tommy's got this habit of getting up in the middle of the night and clearing out the pantry. Joseph woke up one time too many to find us out of the necessities—you know, bread, bacon—"

"Eggs, chicken, ham," Tommy added around a mouthful of chips. "You know, the basics."

"So, anything edible."

"Pretty much," Micah said. "Joseph got this big-assed padlock and locked up the kitchen. You should have heard Tommy. He kept us up most of the night,

48

moaning about hunger pains. It's amazing how much he can whine for such a big guy."

Tommy snorted. "I resent that. I wasn't whining."

Micah clutched his hands to his chest, widening his eyes dramatically. "Oh, God, I'm starving to death. It's been three whole hours since I last ate. How will I ever make it until morning? Oh, woe is me!"

Grady cracked up, almost snorting soda out his nose. "He didn't."

"Oh, I kid you not."

"You're exaggerating," Tommy protested.

"Hardly. The 'woe is me' part is an actual quote, if you may recall."

Tommy shrugged. "All right, so I might have been a little peeved."

"You covered Joseph's bed in mayonnaise."

Grady snorted again, spilling his drink. He grabbed a napkin. When he was finished dabbing, Josh snatched it. He, too, was laughing loudly.

"How much mayonnaise did that take?" Grady asked, still chuckling.

Tommy shrugged, his own smile a bit wild and wicked. "Only about five jars."

"The industrial size," Micah corrected.

"I assume Joseph took the padlock off after that?"

"Nope," Tommy stated cheerfully. "He did yell a lot, though."

"Tommy went in through the window," Micah said.

"Dang near got stuck, too. They just don't make windows big enough these days."

"That's because they expect most sane people to use the door," Micah teased.

"Who said I was sane?"

"You telling that story again?"

Their little group turned, none of them having heard Isaiah and Joseph join the party.

"What story?" Tommy asked innocently, looking at the pair with wide eyes. It was an odd look for him — the man was simply too large and muscular to pull off the innocent look with any success.

"The Great Kitchen War," Isaiah drawled with dry humour.

"Is that what we're calling it now?" Tommy smiled. "I like that, it has style."

Joseph was the only member of the group not smiling. In fact, his scowl was quite fierce. "Don't remind me," he said. "I dang near broke my neck sliding on mayonnaise. It gets damned slippery on top of a wooden floor."

Tommy shrugged. "What can I say? It was a messy job. So I might have spilled a little bit."

"A little —"

"All right, boys, that's enough." Isaiah broke in before the argument could escalate.

Putting Joseph and Tommy together was a little like throwing gasoline on a lit fire. They fed off each other, Tommy doing his best to irritate and Joseph taking the bait. Joseph had quite the temper and no one was able to prick it with quite as much success as Tommy.

Isaiah got Joseph calmed down with the impressive ease of long-standing practice. The rest of their break was spent in companionable conversation. Josh snuggled in next to his big brother when the wind picked up, very much a part of the gang. Grady was proud of his men. They were good guys, one and all, going out of their way to make sure Josh was included in the conversation as much as possible. And Josh, for his part, contributed with his expressive face and even more expressive hand gestures. They should have a game night some time. Josh would be deadly at Charades.

Grady and Josh had grown pretty close lately. They spent the majority of each day together, doing odd jobs around the ranch. Heck, the kid was even helping him out with some of the computer work. Grady didn't do much of it. Isaiah was the ranch's business manager and handled most of the records, finances — all the pesky details that made up Grady's head throb. For only being ten, Josh was amazingly good. He had been helping Grady sort mail and print out schedules. Grady was actually dreading when Josh started school.

It would be quiet around the yard during the day. Lonely. Again.

Isaiah grinned, watching his brother interact with the guys. It was good to see the little boy so happy. In the past two weeks, Isaiah had been getting glimpses into what Josh's life had been like, and he didn't like it. In fact, it made him furious. Josh seemed so eager to soak up any little bit of praise and seemed surprised when anyone included him in conversations or asked his opinion on something. That school of Josh's had clearly done its best, but he'd been shocked to find out exactly how many students attended, most of them year-round. Josh had simply been lost in the shuffle.

Josh was, in Isaiah's opinion, amazing. The kid might not be able to tell stories, but he certainly liked to write them. They would sprawl in the living room at the bunkhouse in the evenings after supper, Isaiah on the couch and Josh in the huge armchair that swallowed his small frame. They'd pull out their battered notebook and talk, Josh writing down his thoughts for Isaiah. Josh had a turn of phrase that never failed to make Isaiah smile, although sometimes that smile was a bit sad, loneliness clear behind the generally light-hearted words.

Josh did pretty darn well with ASL, too. Isaiah, however, was still learning. Isaiah had gone online and loaded up on books and instructional videos to learn sign language, determined to be able to talk to his brother. He was making good progress, although sometimes his motions would send Josh off into fits of laughter.

Grady leaned close, briefly distracting Isaiah with his warm presence. Isaiah had to bite back a groan when he realised he was taking deep breaths. A man who had spent all day in a stable shouldn't smell so good. Arousal was tingling at the base of his spine. Isaiah shifted, completely unsettled, and tried to stuff the feelings back down. He hadn't let his ill-advised attraction to Grady be an issue since the first couple of months he'd worked at the ranch.

"He's settling in real well, isn't he," Grady whispered into Isaiah's ear, the warm breath sending a shiver rippling along Isaiah's skin.

"That he is," Isaiah agreed on automatic pilot. He was just too distracted to be putting together sentences. Everyone else was pretty much finished eating, while he'd barely touched his own lunch. Grady and Josh would head back to the ranch pretty soon.

"Oh," Grady said abruptly. "You got a call this morning from the principal over at Barton. I wrote the number down back at the house."

"Shit, I was waiting for that one." Isaiah pulled his phone out and started scrolling through the call list, hoping he hadn't erased it recently. Unlikely, but he never knew. Ah, there it was.

Isaiah nodded and nudged Josh. "I'm gonna go make a phone call, buddy. Why don't you help Micah clean up?"

Isaiah hopped off the back of the truck, leaving Josh eagerly assisting Micah.

Isaiah strode out of earshot and hit the call button.

He had arrangements to make. Best to quit putting them off.

Chapter Six

Isaiah dropped the box on the floor, his exaggerated groan accompanied by the sound of something breaking. "I think that's the last of it," he said, straightening. He put his hands on his back and stretched. He could fix fences all day and only get a pleasant ache in his muscles. Two hours of hauling junk across the yard and he could barely move.

"I would sincerely hope so," Grady replied dryly. "My question is how the hell did you get all this crap in that small room?"

"Damned if I know," Isaiah replied. It was ridiculous. When he had started packing things up and had realised how much junk he'd accumulated over the last eight years, it was a bit shocking. The closet had been like that fabled bottomless pit. No matter how much he had pulled out of it, more had kept coming. Add in the stuff scattered all over the room he'd been sharing with Josh and he felt like a blasted hoarder. Half of it was probably going straight into the trash when he unpacked, that was for sure.

"You sure about this?" Isaiah asked, probably for the fifth time. He couldn't seem to help it.

"Of course I'm sure," Grady retorted. "The bunkhouse is fine for the guys, but not for a kid. I've got the space. It's logical, damn it, so quit fussing."

Isaiah chuckled. "Right. Sorry. I am fussing, aren't I?"

"Like a damned spinster."

"Gee, thanks." Isaiah laughed again, shaking his head. He shoved a couple of shoe boxes aside with his foot, clearing a path so he could drop onto the bed. "Need help with anything? It's gotta be a bit unsettling, having us move in and take over."

"Nah, it's fine."

Grady looked around the room and shuffled his feet, like he didn't quite know what to do with himself. They'd spent the past couple of hours in enjoyable companionship, but Grady seemed uncomfortable all of a sudden.

"Umm, maybe I'll go see how Josh is settling in," he said.

Isaiah snorted. "The kid escaped to the stables about twenty minutes after we started. He got his DVD collection unpacked and took off."

"At least he's got his priorities straight."

Isaiah laughed again, pleased when Grady joined in this time. The man's laughter had been a bit lacking of late. At first, Isaiah had thought maybe it was because he'd regretted offering them a place, but if anything, his boss seemed eager to get them settled. With that worry put aside, Isaiah had figured Grady was just in one of his moods. It looked like he was right. Isaiah greeted the thought without much relief, though. He didn't like it when Grady was moping. Didn't seem…right, or something.

With school approaching, it had suddenly hit Isaiah—Josh's presence was permanent, not just a summer vacation. Funny how it hadn't really sunk in. At least, not until he started making plans with the school principal. Isaiah loved his life on the ranch, didn't want to quit, and really didn't want to drive in from town every day. But he damned sure couldn't raise a kid in a bunkhouse. When Grady offered them both a place in the main house, Isaiah had taken him up on it. Though he still wasn't certain they weren't being a huge imposition and completely disrupting his boss's life. Again.

"Whatever you're thinking, stop it."

Isaiah looked up sharply at Grady's stern voice. "What are you talking about?"

"You're worrying again. Stop. I wouldn't have offered if I didn't mean it. So quit being an idiot."

Isaiah chuckled. "That might take some doing. I seem to excel at idiocy."

"You do not." The words were harsher and more emphatic than Isaiah's joking intent called for. It startled him and he looked closely at Grady. Grady's face had paled a bit, eyes dark.

Isaiah didn't quite know how to respond. Grady seemed to shake off whatever emotions had gripped him and offered another smile, although this one was still a bit rough around the edges.

"You got time to go over the monthly statements?" Grady asked.

Isaiah let him change the subject—he wasn't quite sure what to do about the earlier conversation, anyway. He really hoped Grady worked through his issues soon. He felt like he had to walk softly around his boss, for fear of stepping on a conversational landmine. And carry a big stick for when the man started talking nonsense.

"Sure. This crap can wait." Isaiah kicked another item in his collection of boxes, giving it a fierce and annoyed scowl.

The two men tromped downstairs and Isaiah slowed his steps a bit so he could ogle. Damn, Grady made a pair of jeans look good. That butt was a thing of beauty.

Isaiah cursed mentally at himself as they entered the study. It was obviously way past time he got laid. The fantasies were taking on a life of their own. Grady might be pretty oblivious most of the time, but even he was bound to notice something soon. Especially if Isaiah kept following him around, drooling over his ass.

The office was technically Grady's, but as the ranch's business manager, Isaiah seemed to spend more time there than anyone. It was a huge room, much larger than either man really needed. Grady had told him once it had actually been two rooms, until he'd had a wall knocked out. The massive L-shaped desk took up nearly half the space, leaving enough room for a long table that doubled as a wet bar and a leather couch. Isaiah had caught Grady sleeping on said couch more than once before. But hell, the thing was more comfortable than a lot of mattresses Isaiah had encountered.

Isaiah dropped into the oversized desk chair, swivelling it until he faced the large computer monitor. Grady perched on the edge of the desk, propping his boot heels on the window sill. It was a setup as familiar as the room itself. They'd spent hours in here, going over strategies and plans. Grady knew the ranching business, inside and out, but he was really weird about touching the computer. As in, he didn't. When Isaiah had first been hired, the records had been a God-awful mess. It had taken him nearly two months just to figure out a system and bring the records up to date. To be perfectly honest, it had looked almost like Grady hadn't even bothered with records at all. How the man had paid his taxes before Isaiah came was anyone's guess.

"So what's the damage this month?" Grady asked.

"Actually, we're looking pretty good. But we need to get the southern herd shipped off. Right now they're just eating up cash."

"How soon can we move them?"

"Not until Joseph gets back." Joseph served more as the foreman than Isaiah did most of the time, but he hated to be solely responsible for decisions. Any decisions. As long as Isaiah was around to give Joseph the go-ahead and approve plans and changes, Joseph did fine. Leave him in charge by himself, and he floundered around like a fish out of water, hemmed and hawed, and generally drove himself — and everyone else — insane second-guessing everything.

Send the man to auction, though, and he was brilliant.

"Do we need to consider adding someone to the payroll?" Grady asked. "It seems like it's been tight around here lately."

"Nah, I think we're fine. We just need to get this last bunch off to market and things will settle down."

"Yeah." Grady stopped talking. Isaiah waited, knowing Grady's silences just as well as his conversation. This was the 'wanting to bring up a difficult topic' silence.

Grady cleared his throat, studying the scuffed tips of his boots. "You know, I've been doing some thinking.

What would you say to not dipping so heavily into the cattle side of things next year?"

"We're a cattle ranch. What, you wanna start breeding ostriches or something? 'Cause if so, I'm gone. I'll wrangle damn near anything, but I draw the line at birds."

As planned, the words forced a startled chuckle from Grady. Isaiah leant back in his chair and fixed his attention on Grady. The big cowboy had that look again, the one that popped up when he started plotting. Fortunately for Isaiah, the man's plots were usually good. And profitable.

Well, most of the time, anyway.

"Look up Esther Farms," Grady said instead of answering. Isaiah obeyed. His mouth swung open.

"Oh, no," he declared. "Hell no. Do you have any idea how much one of those suckers eats? I think I'd rather have the birds."

Grady bit his lip. "I've always liked 'em," he defended.

Isaiah glared balefully at the picture staring up from the computer screen. Heavy muscles and a strong body narrowed into furry feet as the Shire horse stared blankly back at him. "And what, exactly, are we going to do with them?" Isaiah asked pointedly.

"Breed them. Show them. Their numbers drop every year. We're stable financially."

Isaiah looked at the expression on Grady's face and bit back a groan. "Seriously, man?"

Grady looked away, a dull flush creeping up his face.

Shit. Why couldn't Isaiah say no to that look? Damn it, Josh was going to play him like a master in a few years if he didn't toughen up.

Isaiah sighed. "We can talk about it, I suppose. Just...let's get set for the winter first, huh? There's plenty of time before spring to make a decision. And while we might be in the black, no sense digging ourselves into a hole."

"I suppose," Grady murmured.

The look on the big rancher's face was nearly enough to make Isaiah give in right then and there, but he stifled the urge. He was, after all, Grady's business manager. It was up to him to keep Grady from chasing butterflies.

It was his job. Even if it sometimes made him feel about as big as a grasshopper.

Chapter Seven

"Josh!" Isaiah bellowed, planting his hands on his hips and throwing his head back. Silence. He stomped off the porch, muttering to himself.

Isaiah snagged the first person he saw, grabbing Tommy's arm as the big cowboy passed. "You seen Josh?"

"Not lately," Tommy said. "Why, you lose him again?"

"I did not—" Isaiah cut himself off. It wasn't Tommy's fault that Isaiah was in a piss-poor mood.

Of course, the shit-eating grin he received wasn't exactly helping Tommy's cause.

"You're a real jerk, you know that?"

"I aim to please." Tommy grinned again.

Isaiah pinched the bridge of his nose, closed his eyes and tried to rein in his temper. All day he'd been wrestling with legal crap, forms and government regulations. Who knew so much was required just to get a kid into school? It was utterly ridiculous. He had an appointment set up with the principal over at the

Barton school and Josh needed to go with him, but that wouldn't work if he couldn't *find* Josh.

"Just help me look, would you?" Isaiah asked. "And no snarky comments, please. I'm already running late."

"Can't you go without Josh?" Joseph sauntered up and clapped a hand on Isaiah's shoulder. "Barton's a bit of a haul. You could make sure it's what you want to do before you go getting the kid involved."

"I don't really have many options," Isaiah pointed out. "Josh needs to go to school and I'm not about to send him to Edmonton."

Edmonton was the nearest town to the ranch. It was also a place to be avoided, at least in Isaiah's mind. It was full of typical small-town bigotry. No way was he going to expose Josh to that. Word on the street—or rather, according to Grady—was that Barton was a much more liberal, accepting place.

"Besides, the principal mentioned something about tests," Isaiah added. "Joseph, you can help look, too. Josh was supposed to muck out stalls. Start there. And if he didn't finish, Tommy can do it."

Joseph nodded, sent Tommy a glare that said 'behave' and took off.

"Fuck a duck." Tommy scowled. If there was one job the big cowboy avoided, it was stall duty. He claimed they didn't make the rakes long enough for someone of his height.

"Watch your language," Isaiah snapped. He'd made the resolution that they all needed to cut back on the cussing, now that Josh was around.

"Why?" Tommy asked with his patented innocent grin. "It's not like the squirt's gonna pick up the words and start cussing back."

"Tommy!" Isaiah yelled, shocked that Tommy would say something so...hell, he didn't even have the words. *Damn it all, now I'll have to fire the man and Tommy is a good –*

A muffled sound stopped his thoughts dead in their rambling tracks. He looked over in the direction of the small snort. Josh was perched on the fence, fist shoved in his mouth to stifle his laughter. Isaiah didn't know how he'd missed the kid earlier, especially as Josh looked quite comfortable, as if he'd been there a while.

"See?" Tommy said. "The squirt doesn't mind."

Heck, even Grady was smirking. Lungeing a horse in the corral behind Josh, he'd been listening to every word and his amusement was plain.

Isaiah threw up his hands. "Hell, I give up," he yelled.

"Watch your language, boss," Tommy said sombrely.

Isaiah growled. "Come on, Josh," he almost bellowed. "Change your shoes first," he told the kid as Josh passed. "I don't want piles of manure in my truck."

Josh smirked and waved at their audience. Isaiah growled again and stomped off the sound of raucous laughter behind him, deep and booming mingling with high and light. From in front of him, small giggles sounded.

His men were really having a bad influence on Josh. But Isaiah smiled once he was out of sight, anyway.

It took nearly forty-five minutes to make the drive from the Branch to Barton, although part of that had to do with the flock of sheep that had taken up residence in the middle of Jackson Creek Road. Damn smelly, stubborn creatures.

Josh had been uncharacteristically still during the trip—his little body had almost been radiating worry. Even now, as they crossed the nearly deserted parking lot, Josh clung so tightly to Isaiah's hand that his fingers ached. Isaiah suppressed a sigh, knowing any attempt to soothe frayed nerves would be ignored. Again. Hell, Isaiah had talked the whole way here, until his voice started to go raspy. Only time would cure this problem.

Isaiah pulled open the glass-fronted door, ushering Josh inside. Empty schools always gave him the creeps. They echoed and made strange noises and generally freaked him out. Maybe he'd seen one too many episodes of Buffy.

The school wasn't entirely empty, just emptied of students. It wasn't natural—the halls should be crowded and loud, full of kids hurrying places they mostly didn't want to go.

A thin man waited for them on the other side of the double doors. He was short, younger than Isaiah had expected, with a shock of messy brown hair and a bright, friendly smile. Isaiah squeezed Josh's hand and extended the other to greet the man. Tony Malloy, the principal of Barton Elementary School, had a firm handshake, both confident and welcoming. Some of Isaiah's own tension relaxed.

"Isaiah, right? I'm Tony. And this must be Josh." Tony turned his smile onto Josh, who tried to hide behind Isaiah's legs. Isaiah rolled his eyes.

"Yeah, this is Josh. Gotta say, I've never seen him like this. Usually it's all I can do to keep track of him."

"School can be a scary thing," Tony sympathised. "Come on with me and I'll introduce you to Lydia. She'll be Josh's teacher and I do believe she has a few things for him to do while you and I talk."

Josh dug in his heels and refused to move. Isaiah sighed and asked Tony, "Can you give us a minute?"

"Sure," Tony replied. "When you're ready, head straight down the hall, third door on the left, should be the only one open."

Isaiah turned all his attention to Josh, squatting down and tilting that sharp chin up so he could look directly into those familiar green eyes.

"What's wrong, buddy? This isn't like you at all. It's just us here, no other kids, no big deal."

Josh scuffed at the vinyl floor with his toes and stubbornly shook his head.

"Josh, talk to me, please."

Josh looked up and gave Isaiah a venomous glare.

"Oh. So that's it." Isaiah sighed. "I talked to Tony for quite a while on the phone. He says it's not going to be a problem, that Lydia is a great teacher. Your new principal seems like a very nice man, and he assured me they'd do everything they could to help you fit in."

But I never will! The gestures were short, angry. Isaiah tugged the skinny frame in for a tight hug.

"Give it a try, kiddo," he said, running his hand over the baby-soft hair. "I promise, this isn't a punishment. If you really, absolutely hate it, we'll find another option."

They would, too. What that option would be, Isaiah didn't know. He wasn't exactly qualified to homeschool Josh.

He didn't really think it would be necessary. Josh was resilient, with a friendly and outgoing personality. Isaiah had the feeling the boy would fit in just fine, once he got over the newness of it all.

"Come on," Isaiah urged, pulling back. "Today's visit is harmless. You'll meet your teacher, fill out some papers, then we can go home. Grady was talking about us all taking a ride later, maybe hauling some food along and having a picnic."

Hey, Isaiah wasn't above bribing. Not at all.

Josh sighed, his little face serious and looking far too old for his age. Isaiah stood, ruffling the boy's hair, before grabbing his hand again. This time Josh came, albeit slowly, sneakers dragging along the floor.

Tony was waiting inside the classroom with a woman who looked nothing like any teacher Isaiah had had in school. She had short black hair, spiked at the top with deep blue tips. Her makeup was dramatic and she even had a tiny stud in her nose.

Drawings were scattered along the walls of the small room, desks askew. A coat rack in the corner sported one lone, tiny jacket. The building, at least, was average in the extreme. *To make up for its staff*, Isaiah mused wryly.

"Lydia, I want you to meet Isaiah Preston. And this, of course, is his brother Josh."

"Hey, Josh," Lydia said with a bright, welcoming grin. Josh must have liked what he saw, because he waved. And then, to Isaiah's pleased surprise, she repeated her greeting in sign language.

"Lydia started working with a local woman the day I told her about Josh. Between the two of them, they have some wonderful ideas for integrating ASL into the curriculum."

"Wow, that's—"

"Great for the kids, right?" Tony interrupted Isaiah, casting a warning look at him. Isaiah closed his mouth and decided to just go with it.

"Why don't you two go take care of boring paperwork and talk about whatever needs talking about?" Lydia ordered. Gently and sweetly, but it was still an order. "Josh and I will get acquainted."

Isaiah hesitated for a minute, suddenly reluctant to leave Josh alone. But Tony grabbed his arm, agreeing cheerfully, and gave Isaiah no choice but to go along.

A few minutes later and Isaiah found himself in a principal's office for the first time since high school. He squirmed in his chair. Dang, but this brought back memories. Uncomfortable, irritating memories. He couldn't quite get rid of the vague, nagging feeling that he was in trouble. Ridiculous, of course. He was just here to talk to the man about enrolling Josh in school, not to get in trouble for punching Billy Christians in the nose. Not like the little shit hadn't deserved it, after all, but that was damn close to twenty years ago.

Strange, the shit a person remembered when they were nervous.

"You're sure Josh will do okay here?" Isaiah blurted out, searching for reassurance. He was so new at this parenting stuff. Isaiah just knew he was going to screw it all up. *Then Josh will be one of those damn troubled teenagers you see on television and* —

Tony's pen had been scratching madly as he put his signature on some complicated government form, but he paused to give Isaiah a considering look, blessedly cutting off Isaiah's inner tangent into idiocy.

"He'll do just fine here," the principal finally assured Isaiah gently. "Our kids aren't typical."

Before Isaiah could ask for clarification on that odd statement, Tony continued, "May I ask you a somewhat personal question?"

Isaiah shrugged. "Go for it."

"Is there a reason you're putting him here instead of at Edmonton?"

Isaiah paused, but it wasn't really a difficult question. It had taken some doing, and he'd been forced to jump through a couple of hoops to get Josh into the Barton school district. But as the Branch wasn't parcelled out to a school district, and both were funded by the same county, it had ended up being possible.

"I've heard that Barton is a little bit more...accepting than Edmonton."

To Isaiah's surprise, that drew a hearty laugh out of Tony. "I should say so," he finally said. "Edmonton has been around since God only knows. They're pretty traditional."

"Most towns in this area are."

Tony sat back in his chair and tilted his head at Isaiah. "How much do you know about the history of our little town?"

"Not much," Isaiah admitted. "But my boss has lived around here his entire life. He thought Barton might be a better fit for Josh than Edmonton."

"Your boss?"

"Grady."

"Ah, Grady." Tony's face split into a wide grin. "I haven't seen him around here in quite some time. How is he?"

"Fine," Isaiah said with a shrug. He wasn't really surprised that the two men knew each other. The miles between here and the Branch might be considerable, but the number of people wasn't. Edmonton was also a touch smaller than Barton. Isaiah had been known to send his men to Barton on more than a few occasions, when what they needed couldn't be found in the closer town.

"Grady could have benefited from spending more time in Barton. He still could," Tony added the last in a mutter and moved on quickly. "Barton is an eclectic place. You won't find many towns like ours, particularly in such a conservative part of the country."

Thinking of Lydia's offbeat appearance, Isaiah would have to agree.

"Fact of the matter is Barton grew out of a hippie commune that was formed here in the early Seventies."

"Huh." What else could you say to that?

Tony laughed, a rich and amused sound that invited any who heard it to join him. "That is probably the mildest reaction I've ever gotten from that statement."

Isaiah shrugged again. "As long as Josh is treated well, I couldn't care less if it started out as a zoo."

Tony seemed to find that statement hilarious. When he finally got his laughter under control, they went back to the mountain of forms it seemed the government required for just about anything these days.

Isaiah noticed that several times, Tony gave him speculative looks. He brushed it aside, but about the fifth time it happened, he started to wonder if maybe he'd forgotten to shave this morning. He rubbed his chin. Nope. Stubbly, but not bad. So, not a lack of a shave.

When it happened again, Isaiah stared back, arching one eyebrow at the principal.

Tony blushed. "Sorry. I just...oh, hell, I may be completely off here, but I don't suppose you'd be interested in getting some dinner with me sometime?"

Huh. Okay, didn't see that one coming. Josh's new principal was asking him on a date? Barton really was different.

Tony was cute, nice. Normally, Isaiah would have accepted without even thinking about it.

Isaiah found himself shaking his head without making a conscious decision. "You seem really nice, but I'm kind of involved with someone right now. Thanks for the offer, though."

The words popped out and Isaiah could only wonder what the heck was going on in his subconscious. And why the word 'involved' conjured up a picture of a smiling Grady. They weren't involved, weren't a couple. Hell, Isaiah didn't even know for sure that Grady was gay. The man played it too close to the chest for Isaiah to have ever come to a definite conclusion on that one.

Tony was giving him another speculative look, this one followed by a knowing smile. "Cool. Just thought I'd ask. I don't get a lot of hot gay cowboys wandering into my office, you know?"

Isaiah laughed. When he said his goodbyes and collected Josh an hour later, it was with a relieved smile and a much lighter step. Tony and Lydia were realistic—they understood the extra work needed to fit Josh into the school, and were matter-of-fact about dealing with his needs. He had the feeling that between the two of them, there was little that they couldn't handle. They would take good care of Josh and see that he made a place for himself.

Isaiah fired up the truck and pulled out onto the street with a much happier little boy riding beside him this time. That was one worry taken care of.

Only about a hundred more to go.

Chapter Eight

"Well, screw you, then!"

Grady looked up as Isaiah slammed down the phone with a low curse. Peering at the ticked-off man warily from across the room, Grady cleared his throat.

"Problem?" he asked.

"Oh, no, everything's fine." Isaiah sent him a smile, but it looked incredibly fake. "So, Joseph had some thoughts about—"

"Isaiah."

"What?"

"Who was on the phone?"

"It's no big deal, Grady, I swear."

Grady wasn't buying it for a minute. "Isaiah."

"I was thinking about those damned accidental cross-breeds we've got. Jensen said he might be willing to—"

"Isaiah."

"Huh?"

"You tryin' to distract me?"

"Maybe."

"Try harder."

"Boss!"

The bellow bounced off the walls, accompanied by the slamming of the front door. Joseph appeared in the office doorway seconds later. His face was ruddy, and his breathing heavy.

"Boss," Joseph repeated with urgency. "We've got a fence down and cattle wandering into Murphy's pastures."

Isaiah sighed. "All right, I'm coming."

He'd only taken a step when Micah burst through the front door and slid down the hall, nearly crashing into Joseph as he tried to skid to a fast stop.

"'Nother fence down," he gasped. "Brutus and Hector are loose and headin' for the hills. By way of Campbell's place."

"Shit!" Isaiah's face paled with panic. "Damn it to hell, Campbell will kill me if our boys get in with his girls."

"Damn right," Joseph agreed.

Isaiah grabbed his hat off the corner of Grady's desk and was gone before Grady could blink. Grady groaned, grabbed his own hat, and hustled out after them.

It was too damn early to be dealing with crises—barely nine a.m.. The bulls wouldn't wait for Grady to have his third cup of coffee, though. Campbell and him didn't get along at the best of times. If Grady's bulls threw calves with some of Campbell's heifers...well, it wouldn't be pretty. Grady mostly bred mixed Hereford stock while Campbell was extremely picky about the bloodlines of his Black Angus.

Cowboys streamed to the barns—his entire crew including his four main hands and the six temp guys were moving fast. Grady wasn't overly fond of a couple of his temporary employees, but the ranch and pastures needed to be readied for the encroaching winter. Fall was looking to be short this year and his regular crew wasn't going to be able to get the job done. Grady would let the extra workers go in a week or so, but for now, he was extremely grateful they were still around.

Someone had already saddled up Lance for him, so Grady grabbed the reins and hauled ass. He stopped just outside the barn, tightening the girth and zipping up his coat. Grady gathered the reins and had one foot off the ground when something slammed into his side. He went reeling. Lance danced to one side and snorted, panic imminent.

"What the hell?" Grady yanked Lance's head down. He ran one hand over the gelding's side, trying to soothe his boy down.

A mumbled apology reached his ears, and he saw James rush past without stopping. The man didn't look sorry, though. In fact, Grady would have sworn he saw a smirk.

For the love of God, he didn't have time for this. Growling low, Grady swung up in the saddle. Lance pranced a bit more, still worked up. Grady spun him in a circle and urged him forward, putting that nervous energy to better use.

"You, me and Joseph are going after the bulls," Isaiah shouted from atop Tobias. "I'm sending everybody else after the loose herd."

Grady nodded his acknowledgement, guiding Lance through the teeming, barely controlled chaos with practiced ease. Horses and men milled about, the frantic energy making it seem like the crowd in the yard was twice as large as it actually was.

Grady caught up with Joseph, scowling fiercely. "So, how come I've got cattle roaming everywhere but where they're supposed to be?" he snarled. "All at the same damn time?"

Joseph shrugged and wouldn't meet Grady's eyes. "Just bad luck, I guess."

"Bull. Shit."

"Ease off, Grady," Isaiah said in a low voice. "Let's get everybody back where they belong. Then we can worry about the whys and wherefores."

To Grady's complete and utter relief, his two big bulls were moving slow. It took them just a little over an hour to track them down and pen them up. Thankfully without a female in sight.

With the worst crisis behind them, it was off to join the others. Isaiah urged his mount through the busted fence first, Joseph loping past once they hit the other side. Grady hung back, easing his big grey gelding to a halt at the break.

He swung down, eyes scanning the terrain. In the distance, barely visible over the horizon, figures weaved back and forth. Whoops and hollers floated on the wind as men rousted cattle out of the brush.

Grady already knew what he was going to find when he shoved on the post. The break was long, stretching nearly a good hundred feet across the brown grass. Two posts were ripped out, like the herd had hit the fence going top speed.

But they hadn't. Crouching down, Grady cursed silently. The wire had been shredded, cut in multiple places. The posts themselves *had* been ripped out, but going by the tire tracks, it had been done by somebody with four-wheel drive and a couple of thick ropes.

Goddamn it.

Grady shoved back his hat, rubbing at his forehead. As if he didn't have enough to deal with—now they were getting sabotaged.

"What did you find?"

Grady stood, shaking his head. "Deliberate," he spat.

Isaiah sighed heavily. "Why am I not surprised?"

Grady rubbed at his jaw, pissed off and annoyed in equal measures. Goddamn it, why couldn't people leave well enough alone? He stayed mostly to the ranch, kept his head down. Why did they have to push? He remounted, barely keeping his anger under control.

"We'll worry about it later," Isaiah said. "Come on, we've got work to do."

Grady nodded wordlessly and kneed Lance to the left, cutting off an ambling steer. The big dumb critter lowed at him, turning reluctantly. God, Grady hated this. Riding the land, training horses—that was what he loved. The cows, though, drove him nuts. They were big and smelly and stupid and he was a rancher, for God's sake. He wasn't supposed to hate his stock.

James cantered past and Grady saw his mouth move. This time the disgust on the cowboy's face was easy to read. Grady was grateful he couldn't hear the words, certain they were uncomplimentary and bigoted.

Another steer charged, Lance wheeling easily away before cutting off the animal's retreat. After the third time an animal 'got away' from one of his hands, Grady began to detect a pattern.

"Don't get angry," he muttered to himself. "They'll be gone soon."

He only hired extra guys for certain times of year and couldn't claim to know any of them very well. At the moment, he figured that was a good thing. He probably wouldn't like them.

"Steady, boss," Tommy warned as they tag-teamed a pair of worked-up heifers. "We'll be done soon. Then you can give them all the boot."

Apparently, he wasn't the only one noticing the crappy behaviour.

Grady pulled off to one side to give Lance a breather. His eyes sought and found a familiar figure, and a smile tilted the corners of his mouth for the first time in hours. Isaiah and Tobias weaved and dodged, in perfect sync. It was a sight to behold, stirring in more ways than one. Isaiah dodged a mis-flung rope, for once the action not deliberate, and laughter deepened the creases in his cheeks.

Grady's half-smile widened. Now this, he liked. Watching man and horse, breathing crisp air and listening to the sounds of nature — minus the blasted cows, of course.

He wondered if maybe it wasn't time to make some changes. For once, the thought didn't make him feel that guilty panic. Sure, the Grady family had run cattle on this land for damn near three generations. That didn't mean they had to keep running cattle for another three.

The thought hit Grady hard. He didn't have to keep doing this, didn't have to keep pretending. He could stop dealing with the temporary hands, stop dealing with cut fences and wandering herds and...just *stop*.

Why the hell had it taken him so long to realise the truth? No one said he had to be a cattle rancher for the rest of his life. The bank account was healthy and the ranch was turning a profit most years. He had a bit of a cushion, enough to take a few risks. He could sell off the rest of the herd in the spring, start fresh — build the business he wanted, not the one his family had started.

A surge of confidence came from nowhere, swamping over him. They could keep the current horses, do some training. Micah was damn good with the horses and so was Isaiah. Joseph might be at a bit of a loss for a while, but Tommy could handle anything Grady threw at him.

Maybe it was time to get those Shires, whatever Isaiah's objections.

Grady smiled again then let loose a small laugh, garnering some strange looks. But the relief and the certainty were undeniable. For so long Grady had tried to do what was expected of him, trying to make people approve of him. And they never did, never.

So what had changed? It only took a second for the answer to hit Grady. Watching Josh, how brave that kid was...really, Grady couldn't do any less. Isaiah would back him on this — probably after a bit of an argument, but he would support Grady in the end. Josh would be thrilled. The hands would bitch, but they'd adjust. Everyone else could go to hell.

Grady patted the sleek neck below him, running his fingers thought the coarse, tangled mane. "Lance, boy, I think it's time to make some big changes in my life. I think I'm finally ready for it to be *my* life."

Chapter Nine

Isaiah stepped onto the porch, zipping up his coat with gloved hands. The ranch was quiet today, the boys hunkering down inside around the wood stove. Isaiah didn't blame them. The snowstorm that had whipped through the night before had left more than just a thick coating of white on everything. The temperature was down around 'forget the thermometer, I'm freezing my balls off' and any sane person was staying inside beside the nearest heat source.

So what did that say about Isaiah? Probably nothing good. But he was going stir-crazy inside, and if he had to put up with Grady's crappy mood for one more minute, he was going to snap.

Isaiah's sense of fair play took that moment to pop out and remind him that he hadn't exactly been an angel to live with lately, either. He told his inner voice to shut up, but it didn't erase that niggling sense of guilt.

Hell, maybe he just needed to get laid. When was the last time he'd used anything other than his own hand? Isaiah swore softly when he realised he couldn't remember. No wonder he was so cranky.

Grady, on the other hand, was just being difficult.

The screen door squealed behind him and Isaiah's jaw clenched. "Get back inside before you freeze to death," he said around gritted teeth.

"Isaiah."

Isaiah swung around. "What?"

Grady stood in front of the door, hands shoved in his jeans pockets, clad in nothing more than a thick AQHA sweatshirt. Isaiah rolled his eyes. The man really did plan on freezing to death.

"If you're gonna bug me, at least put a coat on," he ordered.

"You want to tell me what's eating at you?" Grady pressed, making no move to go back inside. "Josh is worried."

Isaiah snorted. "Oh, please. He's so absorbed in that new video game you bought him we could blow up the couch and he wouldn't notice."

"What is with you?" Grady demanded. "I've never seen you in such a crappy mood."

"You!" Isaiah whirled around. Everything welled up—the sudden responsibility of Josh, moving in with Grady, their constant arguments lately, the lack of sex. God, the list was endless, and Isaiah snapped.

He ignored the way Grady took a reflexive step back, ending up pressed against the side of the house. Isaiah's temper was in control and it felt damned good. "For the last month you've been wandering around in a daze. You barely talk to me and practically run from the room when I'm around. You spend half your time hiding in your bedroom and last night you fell asleep at dinner. You won't discuss the ranch with me, you won't discuss business plans. I don't know what's going on with you, and you're obviously not interested in sharing. You want to be an antisocial bastard? Fine, but at least have the decency to quit lying to me."

"I'm fine—"

"What the hell did I just say?" Isaiah scowled, planting his clenched fists on his hips and struggling with the urge to throw a punch at that stubborn jaw. Talking to Grady could be like talking to a rock. The man only heard what he wanted to hear, and most of that he chose to misinterpret.

Josh and Isaiah had been living in the big house with Grady for nearly a month now. At first, it had been great. For the first time, Isaiah had felt like he was getting to know the real Grady—a big-hearted man whose laugh stirred equal parts lust and affection in Isaiah. He'd managed to shove back the lust, despite the looks he caught from Grady. They were building a comfortable little makeshift family here and he wasn't about to mess it up by throwing sex into the mix. But just when they'd established a nice routine, Grady had withdrawn.

Grady sighed and shifted from one foot to the other, one toe poking out of a hole in the blue woollen sock. "Can we at least discuss this inside where it's warm?"

"No." Isaiah could be stubborn, too. All right, it would be more effective if he wasn't spiting himself with it, but Isaiah wasn't feeling very rational at the moment.

"Then—"

Josh banged outside, nearly sending Grady flying as the screen door whacked the big man in the ass. Isaiah snickered.

"Where do you think you're going?" he yelled after the figure bundled up in a bright red coat. Josh, at least, had the sense to dress appropriately.

Josh's hand flicked up in a quick gesture. *Barn.*

Isaiah shook his head. He should have known. He let Josh go. It was nearly as warm inside the stable as it was in the house. They kept it shut up tight and all those equine bodies put out enough heat to rival a furnace. It was nice and cosy and would keep Josh occupied for a while.

"Out to the stables?" Grady asked, lips twitching.

Isaiah nodded his head. He started to share a smile with Grady, then remembered that he was mad at the man and turned it into a scowl. Grady scowled back.

"I'm fine, it's not a lie, and you're being a jackass," Grady said. "And I'm not going to stand out here while my toes go numb."

Grady stormed back inside and Isaiah dogged his heels, slamming the door shut behind him. Isaiah instantly started to sweat in his multiple layers. Stripping off his gloves, he tossed them to the floor like an ice hockey player preparing for a fight. The coat dropped next.

"I don't get you," he snarled, still peeling off layers of outer wear and clothing. He hated the cold. Hated it. "You're like that damn downstairs shower when somebody flushes the toilet, hot and cold and back again with no time to take a breath between. One minute I think I understand what's going on inside your head, the next I'm floundering around like an idiot. If you're having problems and you don't want to share, fine." *And it doesn't hurt. It doesn't.* "But you're acting all secretive and odd and it's starting to bug not just me, but Josh, too. He asked me the other day if you were getting tired of us hanging around all the time."

Isaiah's anger abruptly deflated when he looked up and saw the stricken expression on Grady's face.

"He asked what?" Grady asked hoarsely. "No, that's—of course I'm not getting tired of you. That's ridiculous. I like having both of you in the house with me. You know that."

"I don't know a damn thing when you *won't talk to me!*" Fuck, it felt good to yell. Probably counterproductive, but they said repression was bad for your heart, right?

"It's stupid," Grady muttered to his feet. "Really. I'll talk to Josh, though. Let him know it's nothing personal. Both of you, you belong here. I'm not thinking about kicking you out or anything, I swear, and I don't want you guys even thinking something like that."

Isaiah sighed, but the closed-off expression in Grady's eyes told Isaiah he wasn't going to get anything else out of Grady. Not now. If he knew anything for certain about the frustrating man, it was that Grady only shared so much at a time. Then he sealed up tighter than a brand-new pickle jar.

Isaiah shoved his snow-covered boots into the closet, where they could melt without leaving a big puddle that he'd have to clean up. Or, more likely, would slip in and end up on his ass in the hallway. It wouldn't be the first time. Josh was usually pretty good about doing chores when asked, but the brat could never seem to remember to put his boots away.

"Josh will want some hot chocolate when he comes in," Isaiah said. It was a peace offering of sorts, he figured. His anger was gone now and he just felt tired and defeated. Grady didn't trust him and that hurt. A lot.

Grady's face held a mixture of relief and regret as he agreed. Isaiah warmed up some milk while Grady stoked the wood stove in the living room. Then they collapsed on the couch and popped in a movie while they waited for Josh to drag his frozen self back indoors. The silence stretching between them wasn't uncomfortable, but it wasn't pleasant, either. And Isaiah didn't have the first idea how to change it. It seemed like the harder he worked to get close to Grady, the further Grady pulled away. It was by equal turns frustrating and heartbreaking.

Isaiah let the on-screen explosions and Bruce Willis' quips pull his attention away from a situation he couldn't change. But that didn't mean his plans were aborted, only delayed.

* * * *

Josh was bored. Weird. That didn't happen very often living on a ranch. But Tommy was nowhere to be found—and Josh could usually find him. Isaiah had taken off with the other guys earlier today and wouldn't be back until evening. Josh had finished all his chores and had brushed out Speckle, the horse Isaiah had put in his care. He was sick of video games, the computer was acting funny. Bored, bored, bored.

Chewing on his thumbnail, Josh wandered down the hall. A low curse caught his attention and he halted. Oh. Grady was still there.

Josh poked his head around the door of Grady's office, blinking at the sunlight streaming through the big picture window. The man in question sat behind his big desk, head in his hands, muttering softly to himself.

He didn't want to scare the big rancher, so Josh knocked on the open door. Grady's head went up, expression guilty, as if he'd been caught doing something he shouldn't.

"Josh!" Grady exclaimed. "What are doing in here?"

Josh shrugged and wandered into the room, trailing his fingers along a shelf on the towering dark wood bookshelf against one wall. His sock-clad feet made no sound on the carpet as he circled the room, trying to come up with some excuse for interrupting Grady. Grady sighed heavily, then beckoned to him.

"Come over here, squirt. I could use some help."

Josh bounced over and rounded the corner of the desk. Grady swivelled his chair and pulled Josh in closer.

Oh. Pretty. Josh traced the magazine with one finger, the pages open to display a series of pictures of a big, stocky black and white horse. One photo in particular caught his eye. A horse was racing across a field, the thick white hair on its feet flying, mane whipping around the massive head, big brown eyes shining with life and excitement.

"He's a beauty, isn't he?" Grady agreed in a low voice.

Josh nodded.

"They're called Shires. You don't see them much anymore. They were originally bred to carry knights into battle a long time ago. Then people used them for farming and logging and hauling cargo in wagons. But since tractors came along, the big breeds are slowly dying out. People are doing their best to help, but it's not easy. I love them, always have."

Josh pursed his lips. He'd never seen that particular look in Grady's eyes. He switched his attention from Grady to the magazine then back again. If Grady liked the big horses so much, why weren't there any on the ranch?

Josh did his best to ask that exact question. It took a minute, but Grady caught his meaning. His smile was tinged with sadness and his voice, when he spoke, grated with a tone that sounded like rust and dirt.

"This is a working ranch. A Shire isn't a practical addition. They aren't good for herding cattle and not much needs hauling that we can't do with the tractor, truck, or ATVs."

Josh might have been young, but it sounded a lot like Grady was quoting someone else. Snatching a piece of paper off the corner of the desk, Josh quickly scrawled, '*Who says you always have to be practical?*' He handed the sentence to Grady and the man took it, but didn't look. Instead, he faced Josh with a solemn face.

"Isaiah says you're feeling a bit uncomfortable around me," he said slowly.

Josh shrugged. Not uncomfortable, exactly. He just felt like half the time, when he tried to communicate with Grady, that Grady wasn't interested in deciphering Josh's meanings.

Grady scrubbed at the darkening stubble on his chin. "I know I'm not always easy," he admitted. "But you and Isaiah are the only family I have."

Huh. That was a new one. Josh poked at the paper, wanting to know why Grady hadn't tried to read it. Grady handed it back with a sad downward tilt to his lips.

"I can't read." The words were spoken so softly that Josh almost missed them.

Josh's eyes widened at the confession. He poked at Grady's hand and, when that didn't work, grabbed the man's face in both of his hands and made Grady look at him. He let the silence stretch, knowing Grady could read the questions in his eyes.

"One of my teachers in grade school thought I might be dyslexic," Grady finally said. "I could never make the letters behave. They always turned around and upside down and got all mixed, even when I was just trying to learn the alphabet. I dropped out of school in eighth grade and no one really cared. No matter how hard I try, even now I can only make out really simple things like headlines and signs, or sentences that I'm really familiar with. You know, invoices that I see every day, that sort of thing."

Oh. Wow. Josh wouldn't have even guessed. Grady looked so sad and miserable that Josh just had to lean in and give out a hug. His arms couldn't reach all the way around the bulky chest and Grady was hard and solid to his touch. The big frame stiffened for a second, but just as Josh was going to pull away, Grady lifted his arms and squeezed Josh close.

"Thanks, kiddo," he said in a gruff voice. "You're the only one besides my sister who knows. I don't want it getting out, ya know? Wouldn't do for people to know that a local business owner can't read. They try to cheat me often enough as it is."

Josh's eyes narrowed. Why would people try to cheat Grady? People had generally been pretty nice to Josh.

Grady changed the subject. "I never meant to make you feel like I wasn't listening. I can't always follow along, though, you know?"

Josh rolled his eyes and smacked Grady lightly on the shoulder. Silly man. He should have told Josh earlier, then they could have worked something out already. Josh was good at hand signals, he'd had a lot of practice over the years. So, he'd need to remember to use them more around Grady. No big deal.

"Think you could do something for me?"

Josh nodded eagerly, wanting to erase some of the sadness from Grady's eyes.

"My father would never let me add any Shires to the ranch, but he's not in charge anymore, is he? I was thinking the other day that there's no reason why I can't now. Would you be willing to do some research for me? Learn more about the breed, and maybe find out about some of the breeders in the area. You're a whiz on that computer and I think, if I went in armed with information, it'd be easier to talk Isaiah into this."

Josh cocked his head.

"He's my business manager, kiddo," Grady clarified. "I might own the place, but he approves most of the purchases. Heck, I really ought to make him a full partner, he already does the work. And with you here, I want to make sure he always has a place, huh?"

Wow, again. Josh had heard the guys, including Isaiah, talk about Grady sometimes. They always called him things like aloof, a loner, hard to know. They said he kept to himself and was a gruff old bear. But that wasn't what Josh saw, not at all. He didn't see a loner, he saw someone lonely. Gruff, but he did it to keep himself from being hurt. Josh knew about that, he really did. He'd used his lack of speech on more than one occasion, to keep people at bay. New and short-term stepfathers. Well-meaning teachers. His mother.

Josh made sure Grady looked at him before picking up the magazine to let Grady know he would help in any way he could. Then he mouthed carefully, "*I love you.*"

Grady's eyes went wide with shock and turned dark, shimmering a bit. Then a slow smile began to spread across his face until he favoured Josh with the happiest look he'd ever seen on the rancher.

"I love you, too," Grady replied.

Abruptly, Grady stood, moving Josh out of the way so he didn't get knocked over. "Enough serious stuff," he declared. "I think some cookies are in order. Want to help? If we start now, we'll be able to eat some before Tommy gets his hands on them."

Josh giggled, nodding. He took Grady's hand and tugged him down the hall, both of them sharing a conspiring smile.

Chapter Ten

Isaiah lunged for the phone, grabbing it just before the answering machine picked up. His greeting was a bit breathless, but what could you expect from someone who'd done a mad dash across the house and leapt across the room? Grady really needed to put a phone in another room besides the kitchen and his bedroom. The living room would be nice. Like most normal people.

A long stretch of silence greeted his voice. Isaiah was about to hang up when he finally got an answer.

"Who the hell is this?"

The female voice was belligerent, sharp, and strangely familiar. Isaiah racked his brain for a connection even as he replied.

"This is Isaiah. What can I do for you?"

"Where's Dillon?"

"Who?"

"Dillon. You know, the idiot who owns that hellhole."

Okay, Isaiah was seconds away from hanging up. "We don't have a Dillon here," he said coldly. "Check your phone number."

"Oh, please. As if I'd misdial this number. And I know Dillon is there. You'd have to pry him off that place with dynamite."

A hand on his shoulder made Isaiah jump. Dang. He'd been so absorbed in the irritating conversation he hadn't heard Grady come into the room.

Grady silently held his hand out for the phone and Isaiah passed it over without argument.

"Yeah?"

Isaiah turned and was nearly out of the room when Grady's words made him freeze.

"What now, Tracy?"

Tracy? Wait, that...Dillon? Grady? Well, hell. Isaiah felt about as big as a lizard when he realised he hadn't remembered Grady's first name.

"Tracy, I can't...why don't you just..." Grady gave a sad, resigned sigh. "All right, how much?"

Isaiah was eavesdropping shamelessly, but he didn't care. He didn't like how that girl had spoken to him on the phone, and he really didn't like the sound of defeat in Grady's voice.

"You'll have the money in a couple of days. But why don't you —"

Grady's hand tightened around the handset until his knuckles went white. Then he replaced the receiver with exaggerated care.

"Anything I can do?"

Grady's eyes widened as he whirled around on stocking feet, obviously unaware that Isaiah was still there. "Oh. It was just Tracy."

"Who's Tracy?" Isaiah felt guilty that he even had to ask. That feeling increased with Grady's answer.

"My sister."

"You never really talk about her," Isaiah observed.

Grady shrugged. "We don't get along so well. She pretty much only calls when she needs money."

"That sucks."

"Yeah, it does."

Grady shifted, clearly wanting to drop the subject. Isaiah wasn't prepared to let him, though. He leaned against the doorjamb and blocked Grady from fleeing.

"Want to talk about it?"

"No."

"I think you need to."

"Don't care."

Isaiah couldn't help but grin at the petulant tone that crept into Grady's words.

"You sure?" he teased gently.

"Yep."

Damn. He half expected the man to thrust out his lower lip and start pouting. This time Isaiah chuckled out loud.

"All right. I'll let it go. This time." He kept his tone light, but the words were a warning. Now that Isaiah realised how badly he'd behaved around Grady, he was damn well determined to fix it. Whether Grady liked it or not.

The expression on Grady's face said 'not'. But Isaiah wasn't going to be put off by that prickly attitude. He'd spent far too much time being offended lately as it was.

"Come on," he said, shoving upright. "The whole reason I came inside was to find you. It's about time to pick up Josh, and I thought you might want to tag along. We could grab some dinner, maybe catch a movie. Something fun to celebrate the end of Josh's first week of school."

Grady hesitated, though yearning was clear on his face. "I wouldn't want to—"

"Shut up," Isaiah said cheerfully. "It'll be fun."

Grady finally nodded. "Let me get cleaned up first," he said in lieu of agreement.

Isaiah took in the stains on Grady's jeans and the large hole in the big toe of his right sock and laughed. "Might not be a bad idea. You've got five minutes."

As Grady disappeared up the stairs, Isaiah went to gather their coats. He was a man on a mission—Grady was going to have some fun for once. No matter how hard he fought it.

Surprisingly enough, there was a minimal amount of stubbornness to overcome. Grady came along almost peacefully and the drive was pleasant. He greeted Josh with a big smile and didn't argue over the movie choice. He even seemed to enjoy it.

Josh, on the other hand, was clearly having a blast. He was still giggling incessantly as they exited the theatre. Isaiah looked over at Grady to see the barely contained mirth in the his eyes.

The movie had been an action flick, albeit a pretty tame one. Josh seemed to think it was a comedy, though. The kid had laughed hysterically through every—mostly non-violent—death scene. Isaiah was just glad the theatre had been pretty empty, or they might have been kicked out. Josh's laughter was like an infectious disease—it never failed to set off his companions.

Grady grabbed Josh's hand as they prepared to cross the street. The little family-style restaurant they were aiming for was only half a block from the movie theatre. The weather was mild enough today that it wasn't worth driving and trying to find somewhere else to park.

"You know," Grady teased, "I don't think the director would appreciate your attitude towards running a train into the side of a building."

Josh waved expansively with his free hand, fingers moving rapidly. Isaiah laughed.

"The train looked like the model set he has at home," Isaiah translated. "Complete with manufacturer's label."

Grady snorted. "Yeah. Big budget it wasn't."

Enjoyable, though. In fact, Isaiah couldn't remember the last time he'd had this much fun, even if the movie had been crappy.

He paused to hold the glass door open for Grady and Josh. He gratefully welcomed the blast of heat in the entryway. Isaiah figured he'd probably have to retrieve the truck and pick up Josh on the way home instead of walking. Once the sun went down, the temperature went from not quite pleasant to downright uncomfortable.

They found seats at a booth in the back corner. Josh hesitated for a second. Isaiah almost questioned the strange look his little brother gave Grady. Before he could say anything, though, Josh slid in next to the big rancher.

"Gee, guess I'm not good enough anymore," Isaiah teased.

He could have kicked himself when Grady actually looked concerned. "I could —"

Josh broke him off with a quick motion of his small fingers. Isaiah's mouth dropped open.

"Josh! Where the hel — heck did you learn that one?"

Best not to cuss while berating Josh for doing the same.

Josh shrugged, but his lips curved up a bit. He pretended to study the menu with rapt attention. Isaiah groaned.

"Tommy," Grady suggested.

"Probably the first thing he did," Isaiah agreed. "Looked up naughty words in sign language."

They shared a laugh, Isaiah not really able to be angry over it. The kid was growing up in ranching country. In the scheme of things, there were far worse habits he could pick up than a couple of dirty words.

He couldn't quite shake the image of Grady's earlier reaction, though. Didn't the man know when he was being teased? Sure, Isaiah knew Grady tended to take things far too seriously, but maybe he needed to have a talk with the guys about trying to loosen up around the big boss. Isaiah knew he was as guilty as anyone. It only firmed up his resolve to lose some of his assumptions about Grady's attitudes.

"What are you hungry for?" Isaiah asked.

Josh bounced a couple of times on the plastic bench cushion. He flipped the menu around, pointing. Isaiah had to lean over and squint to read the tiny print.

"That's a lot of food for such a tiny body," he commented.

Josh raised one eyebrow.

"Right. Burger platter it is."

When Josh sat back in his seat, Isaiah noticed that Grady's grip on his menu was a bit tight. Huh. He didn't think burger platters were upsetting.

Isaiah glanced over his own menu. Across the small table, Josh leaned against Grady's arm, tugging the menu until it nearly hid his small face. Josh busied himself pointing to different items. Grady made small humming noises of agreement, a smile replacing his earlier almost grim expression. Isaiah had noticed lately that the two of them had come up with their own communication methods. It wasn't ASL, or even Josh's preferred written conversation. But the two of them seemed to understand each other just fine. It pleased Isaiah. A lot. It was nice to see both of them so happy.

The waitress came and they placed their orders. Isaiah thought it was kind of cute, the way Grady ordered exactly the same thing as Josh. Although, knowing Josh, half of Grady's food would probably go into the kid, too. And if it didn't? Heck, Isaiah could always find room for more food.

While they waited, Isaiah and Grady exchanged casual conversation, Josh listening intently and adding his own opinion on occasion in his own special way.

Stares were boring into Isaiah's back, though. He tried to ignore it. Not like he wasn't used to the dirty looks and the disapproval. Of course, if they started anything with Josh around, his temper would probably snap.

Isaiah kept his thoughts to himself. No sense in borrowing trouble. Or looking for some. It would probably find him eventually, anyway.

Chapter Eleven

Grady hit pause and tossed the remote onto the table. He leant forward, rubbing his eyes and feeling like an idiot. He'd been watching these stupid videos of Isaiah's for nearly two weeks and he'd made absolutely zero progress. Grady would think he'd finally got a sign right, only to realise he was doing it backwards, or upside down. Hell, even his letters were generally wrong, and most of the boys had picked those up in mere days. The letters should have been pretty fool-proof. It wasn't like they weren't similar to the written alphabet.

Then again, Grady had never done well with that, either. He'd thought about giving up at least a dozen times. But then he'd see those green eyes in his mind, the ones that, on occasion, saw more than they should.

His hand hovered over the remote again before he pulled it back. Maybe he should call it quits for the night. He was tired and the instructor's words weren't making sense anymore.

"So that's where my tapes went."

Grady jerked, butt sliding on the worn leather couch cushion. He jumped to his feet and turned. Damn it. Isaiah stood at the foot of the stairs, just out of range of the living room lights. The shadows masked his expression and hid the emotions in his eyes.

"I was just—"

"Grady."

At Isaiah's soft word, Grady snapped his mouth shut. Not like the man couldn't see what Grady was doing, anyway. Just because Grady was stupid didn't mean Isaiah was, too.

Isaiah dropped onto the sofa next to Grady, so close their legs brushed. Grady looked away to hide the sudden heat in his face.

"This instructor isn't the best," Isaiah commented, nodding at the figure frozen on the screen across the room.

Grady still couldn't think of anything to say. He took refuge in his usual silence.

Isaiah sighed. "I don't get you," he said. "You act so gruff and aloof all the time, then I find something like this." His wave included the papers scattered all over the table—frozen shots of different signs with the corresponding words.

Grady shrugged. He finally found his voice, although the heat in his cheeks still lingered. "If he's gonna live here, I figured I should try and learn at least a little."

"You know Josh doesn't expect you to," Isaiah pointed out. "He doesn't mind writing things out. In fact, I sometimes think he prefers it. It's easier for him to get out exactly what he wants to say."

"He shouldn't have to. He's family and I don't want him to ever think differently. He needs to know that he fits."

Isaiah sat back, surprise on his face. "Family? Grady, we're just a couple of guys you took in. You don't have to —"

"You're family," Grady cut in irritably. "You live here, you work here, hell, I've known you for damn near a decade." Grady stood, scowling fiercely. "You're family. Both of you. And if I have to bust my ass to learn this stuff, I'll do it, because Josh should never feel like an outsider, or like he doesn't belong."

"Is this what you've been hiding?" Isaiah asked, rising to his feet. They stood toe to toe, identical fierce expressions boring into each other. "Why the hell didn't you just tell me? Or even more, ask for my help?"

Grady looked away, really not wanting to answer that question.

"Grady!" Isaiah shouted.

"Shut up," Grady whispered vehemently. "You'll wake Josh."

"Right now, I don't give a damn. You say we're family, but that goes both ways, you know? You have to let us in sometimes. Don't you think Josh would love to help you with this? That I would?"

"You just don't understand."

"No, I don't. So help me to."

"I can't." The admission sunk into his gut and settled there, making bile rise in his stomach. If Isaiah ever found out... Grady was used to the looks from people. He could handle the mixture of disgust and pity and the name-calling. But not from Isaiah. Never from Isaiah.

He couldn't deal with this anymore. Ignoring Isaiah's calls, Grady turned and stalked off, growly and frustrated and...hurt. Isaiah should know better by now. His guys were all he had. His guys and now

Josh. Grady knew what it felt like, to always be on the outside watching a world where you didn't fit, no matter how much you longed to. And he would go toss himself off Pearson's Cliff before he ever let Josh feel like that.

He snagged his coat and slammed out of the house to lick his wounds, conscious of Isaiah's penetrating stare boring into his back the entire way. It was a relief to make it to the porch and out of sight.

As he always did when he was upset, Grady headed for the barn. He made straight for the stall on the end, letting himself in. Dixon ignored his entrance, shifting his weight on three legs and chewing idly on a mouthful of hay. Grady braced his back against the wooden wall near the door, sliding down until he sat in the newly cleaned woodchips. He braced his arms on his upright knees, tilted his head back, and stared with blank eyes at the rafters above.

He'd screwed up. Again. Damn it. That seemed to be the story of his life. Open-mouth-insert-foot Grady — that was him.

He closed his eyes, letting the soothing sounds of Dixon nearby ease him. He kept trying and trying. And it never made a difference. Hell, most of the time, no one even noticed his efforts. If they did, they chalked it up to some weirdness on his part.

Ever since Grady took over the Branch from his father, he'd been attempting, in his own way, to turn the men here into the family he'd never had. He wanted to fit, so desperately. But it seemed like he could never get past the whole 'boss-employee' divide.

It was probably about time for him to accept that he never would. Grady had hoped, with Isaiah and Josh staying with him, that things could be different. That he could finally get close to the man that he had lusted after from afar since the first time they had met. Maybe, if it had stayed lust, he could have made a move. But Isaiah was so confident and sexy and it hadn't taken long for Grady's feelings to deepen.

Unfortunately, Isaiah still saw him as the boss, just like all the rest. Grady cursed himself as his eyes stung a bit. He shoved to his feet and grabbed Dixon's halter. Maybe a ride would help clear his head.

Dixon was used to their late-night antics and accepted the interruption to his lazy time with equine equanimity. Five minutes later, Grady trotted out of the yard. The trees quickly swallowed them up, encasing Grady in a silent, isolated world that was all his own.

Maybe, for a little while, at least, he could leave everything behind. It had never worked before, but Grady had never been this determined before, either. He was sick of hurting, sick of feeling like an outsider. It was long past time that he became as hard and unfeeling as everyone thought him.

He spurred Dixon into the night, relishing the feel of the wind rushing through his hair. These night rides, surrounded by the peace of the land he loved, were the only times he felt free. Felt like there was somewhere in this lonely world where he belonged.

Chapter Twelve

The music pounded and the lights flashed and damn but if Isaiah wasn't getting a headache. He scowled down at the half-empty beer glass in his hand and wondered when he'd started getting old. A little cutie sashayed past with a big smile for Isaiah, naked from the waist up. Isaiah barely glanced at the creamy skin on display.

Fuck it.

He downed his beer, slammed his glass onto the wet and stained counter beside him and shoved off his stool. Isaiah had come here for a little stress relief and that was exactly what he was going to get. So what if no one here really appealed to his suddenly extremely particular tastes? He didn't have to feel a life-long connection to a guy in order to get his dick sucked.

Isaiah waded into the throng of sweaty, writhing bodies, his eyes scanning for someone who would at least interest his body, if not the rest of him.

The hour-long drive to his favourite dive had seemed like more of a hassle this time than usual. Not technically a gay bar, the place was certainly gay-friendly. Girls in skimpy skirts mingled freely with guys in overly tight pants. If most of the girls seemed more interested in making out with each other than any of the guys on display, well, that was their business. After all, Dave's was one of the few places around where same-sex couples could hook up without getting the shit beat out of them.

The large bar and nightclub had been Isaiah's stomping ground for longer than he cared to remember. When the pressure of celibacy started to get to him, he took a night off and drove out looking for a little companionship. Normally, it took several months before he felt compelled.

He'd been here less than two weeks ago.

Isaiah blamed it on Grady. His attraction for the other man was getting out of control. So he'd had the brilliant idea of coming out and finding some company for the night. Work out some of the sexual tension. Judging by the evening so far, it wasn't going to be overly successful.

Isaiah crossed the room with difficulty, suffering several gropes, more than a few pinches and one slap. His ass was gonna be technicolour in the morning. Place was a goddamned meat market, and why the hell did that suddenly leave such a sour taste in his mouth?

Isaiah propped himself against the far wall and tried not to scowl too ferociously. It was a bit counterproductive, to battle across the room only to play social outcast again. He just couldn't seem to summon the effort to go prowling. Instead, his mind kept drifting back to the ranch.

Why the fuck was Grady suddenly consuming his thoughts? They'd lived and worked together in harmony for so long now. Like brothers.

Cut the bullshit. You never felt brotherly towards the man.

Isaiah cursed his conscience. Couldn't he at least be allowed to lie to himself? Sure, he'd been attracted to Grady at the beginning, but the man was his boss. It hadn't been easy, but Isaiah had fought hard – and won. Admittedly, it helped that he didn't spend a lot of time with Grady that wasn't work-related. Even then, the rancher tended to keep to himself, both physically and emotionally. After a while, it had become second nature to ignore any remaining sparks between them. With the distance between them, both figuratively and literally, he'd managed to shove the attraction into a dark corner and tie it up for a while. Every so often it would rise up again, usually when Grady did something utterly sweet and unexpected, but Isaiah had always been able to rope the sucker back in.

Then came Josh. Living in the same house as Grady, though, was proving to be a bit more than his willpower could handle. He couldn't get that distance needed, the time away from Grady, to hog-tie his crush back up.

Day in, day out, Grady was always there. Invading Isaiah's mind, permeating his thoughts, constant personal interaction making it impossible for Isaiah to keep Grady locked away in his little box. The box Isaiah had constructed and slapped with the label 'boss' and, occasionally, 'friend'. Ever since he had blurted out that strange comment to Tony, though, the label kept insisting on changing itself to 'boyfriend', 'partner'. Isaiah's mind kept insisting of forming distracting images. *Tangled sheets and sweaty skin and* –

Isaiah cut off his thoughts with brutal forcefulness. God, those images were starting to drive him insane. Hence, tonight's outing. Which was proving more pointless with every passing second.

In the next fifteen minutes, at least five men – and three women – passed by, any one of whom he knew would have gladly taken him up on an offer for some fun. The words wouldn't come. Isaiah knew he looked a bit like an idiot, huddling against the wall like some wide-eyed, clueless virgin on his first foray into the world.

Isaiah contemplated leaving. He was just disgusting himself.

A body bumped into him, nothing unusual, but something about the scent of this one caught his attention. *Deep and musky, with the slightest hint of hay and horse. Like* –

Isaiah cut the thought off before it could finish forming. Instead, he summoned his best smile and flashed a wink at the man passing by. The dark-haired guy paused, returned the appreciative look, and gave a quick nod.

Isaiah pushed away from the wall and followed a tight ass, nicely framed by a pair of well-worn jeans. He forced his mind to go blank. And he absolutely, positively, would *not* feel guilty. He had no reason to. He and Grady weren't involved, no matter what that stupid fucking label kept insisting on.

The bathroom was crowded and Isaiah wrinkled his nose. The older he got, the less these hook-ups appealed. It was on the tip of his tongue to ask the guy to go somewhere. Isaiah could find a hotel for the night or something. He didn't really want—

"How 'bout a little more privacy?"

Isaiah turned his head, meeting a heated blue gaze. The brunet smiled and a crooked front tooth presented an oddly charming appearance.

"Seems a little crowded, don't it?" The cowboy slid one hand along Isaiah's arm, the touch hot through the fabric of Isaiah's shirt, sending a little jolt of arousal straight to his crotch. "Why don't we go find somewhere quieter?"

"Sure." Isaiah nodded and licked his lips, raking his gaze over the other man. Long, lean, the build of someone whose cowboy garb wasn't a fashion statement. Those big, callused hands worked for a living, scarred and battered like Isaiah's own.

"Sure," Isaiah repeated. "Lead on."

Isaiah followed that ass back out of the bathroom and down a narrow hallway, emerging through a side door into the chilly night air. The metal door clanged shut, cutting off the laughter and music and leaving a shocking, almost uncomfortable, silence.

"Damn, but you're a sight." This time it was the cowboy who licked his lips and eyed Isaiah up and down. "We're gonna have us some fun, I think."

Isaiah summoned a smile and reached out. He hooked a finger in the brunet's belt and tugged the man closer. He ran his palm down the front of tight-fitting jeans, feeling the bulge and heat of a nice-sized package.

"Sure," he said again. "Fun."

The guy didn't even bother with a kiss. One minute they were checking each other out, the next Isaiah's pants were halfway down his legs and a hand was inside his underwear. He stifled a groan and let his head fall back, bracing himself against the side of the building. They were well-hidden, no one else around. The touch felt so good.

Guilt tried to surge again and Isaiah batted it down. He braced his legs, balls drawing up as that touch sent blood rushing to his cock. Good. He didn't need it in his head right now. Thinking was vastly overrated.

"Mmm, bit distracted, there." The cowboy pulled his hand free and rubbed Isaiah through the dampening fabric of his briefs. "Can't have that, now, can we?"

Without another word, the guy loosened his grip and dropped to his knees. Isaiah moaned loudly when a wet mouth rubbed against his still-trapped cock, the heat nearly unbearable. Cool air hit his skin, making him shiver violently.

Isaiah looked down at that dark head, felt the stranger's hands braced on his thighs. Arousal wanted to swamp him, wanted to take over completely.

He thought he was going to be sick.

Gasping for air, Isaiah put his hands on the man's shoulders and shoved. The cowboy sat back, gaze annoyed.

"What the hell now?"

"I can't do this." Isaiah found his uncertainty sliding away, the doubts that had been plaguing him all night were silenced. "I'm sorry, man, but I can't."

For a minute, Isaiah thought he was going to have a fight on his hands. The man's hands tightened on his thighs, his lips thinning. Then the brunet seemed to rein himself in. He stood quickly, wiping off his hands.

"Whatever, man."

Isaiah thought he heard the words 'cock-tease' as his potential hook-up stalked off in annoyance. Isaiah sighed heavily, part relief, part frustration. Hell. He hadn't been laid in ages — the last trip had been just as fruitless—and here he was leaning against a wall, freezing his ass off in the cold, with his dick hanging out of his pants.

He was an idiot. A total and complete idiot.

Isaiah cursed. He stuffed his cock back in his jeans, ignoring the discomfort when he zipped back up. He deserved it. That, and more. Fuck, his head was a goddamned mess.

Yeah, he thought again. *I'm an idiot.*

Making his way back inside, Isaiah added, *An idiot who's about to get really, really drunk.*

Chapter Thirteen

Isaiah wrote another note on his list, biting his lip as he tried to think of anything else they might need. His head gave a protesting twinge as his brain tried to make sense of the messy scrawl on the paper. He was still feeling the slight effects of a lingering hangover from the night before. He'd stopped drinking at about eleven, crashed in his truck overnight, then had driven back in the wee hours of the morning.

He really, really wanted to go back to bed. It had started snowing on his way back, though, and there was too much to do. He couldn't take a sick day, especially not when it was his own stupidity that was making him sick.

The snowfall had finally tapered off around late morning and the sun had emerged. Little by little, the snow was melting away. Big drifts still nestled against buildings and fence lines, but the roads were clear. They had a few weeks, hopefully, before the snow would stick around.

Joseph had run into Edmonton to pick up their feed order the day before, but more was needed. Two of their mares had decided to pop out late foals, with a third showing signs of carrying, as well. Isaiah was gonna have a long talk with the boys about that one. She wasn't supposed to be bred just yet, and certainly not until spring. Damned if he could figure how it happened, but now he needed additional supplements and the feed wasn't going to last. Add to that and someone—Isaiah wasn't naming names, curse Tommy's hide—had miscalculated on the amount of woodchips stored away. Isaiah had already made three passes through the main barn and the breeding barns and added something to his list every time. Dang thing was nearly two pages long. Of course, his handwriting was on the large side, but still...

"Boss, maybe you should let me go into town for you today." Joseph shifted his weight uncomfortably, breaking into Isaiah's thoughts. He'd been tagging along with Isaiah, helping make plans, pointing out any shortfalls in stock, and bringing him up to date on some of the piddling little issues Isaiah hated dealing with.

"Why should I do that?" Isaiah was only half paying attention to Joseph. He scanned the list again, trying to see if he'd missed anything else.

"It's just, there's talk again and it might be better—"

With that comment, Joseph gained Isaiah's full attention. He looked up, his stern glare cutting Joseph off mid-sentence.

"Don't be an idiot," he snapped.

Joseph obviously wanted to keep protesting but knew better. It wasn't like they hadn't covered this ground before.

Isaiah had never hidden the fact that he was gay. He didn't go around telling everyone and their daughter, but his trips to Dave's were a dead giveaway. Everyone for six counties knew what went on there. Since his sexuality didn't bother Grady, Isaiah figured nothing else really mattered.

But every now and then, the conservative townspeople of Edmonton got riled up about it, usually after one of Isaiah's recreational trips reminded them. It mostly just annoyed Isaiah. He had a thick hide—he could ignore the slurs and insults and glares easily enough—he was used to it. And he could more than hold his own physically, although it rarely came to that. When the tempers were up, he was always careful to stick to public places. The biggest bigots were mostly cowards. They'd jump him in an alley but they weren't about to attack him in full view. Even if no one would fuss about it—too much.

"At least let me go with you."

"Fine," Isaiah said. "Go let Grady know we're leaving."

"Will do, boss." Joseph leapt to obey and Isaiah sighed, pinching the bridge of his nose. Lately, his men couldn't get away from him fast enough. Grady, too. They were both acting like asses and knew it, but the tension between them was out of control lately. Ever since that blasted argument. Isaiah had hoped to ease some of the tension with last night's trip, but obviously that hadn't panned out quite as planned.

After that one time, Isaiah hadn't caught Grady studying ASL again. Grady and Josh were getting along like the best of friends, though, and on the surface, all was well.

Isaiah was just waiting for the next disaster to crop up. The simmering tension hadn't exploded yet, but it was only a matter of time. If bigoted townspeople were it? Bring it on. That was familiar. That he could handle. It was the emotional crap that was kicking his ass.

"Ready, boss."

Isaiah nodded curtly to Joseph and they climbed into the truck. At the last second, Josh came tearing out of the barn, waving madly.

"Looks like someone wants to come with us," Joseph said wryly.

"Yeah. Not sure it's a good idea."

Joseph shrugged. "Can't hurt. Certain people in Edmonton can be bastards, but maybe a kid will curb their tongues some, huh?"

Isaiah wasn't too sure about that but as he wasn't hiding, it wasn't fair to make Josh hide, either. Josh understood that Isaiah was different, as much as it was possible for a ten-year-old to understand. Isaiah and Joseph would both be there to keep an eye on him and make certain no one said anything too nasty in his hearing. And Joseph might have a point. A kid around might keep some people in check. Isaiah should have felt guilty about that but he didn't. Josh loved going into town, particularly if they were headed to Feed 'N Tack. The owner, Carl Evans, had taken a liking to Josh and the feeling was mutual.

Isaiah nodded his consent and Joseph clambered in the truck before scooting over to the middle. Josh climbed in after him, plopped down in the passenger seat, and buckled up. Then he looked over with a huge grin and Isaiah immediately felt his mood lighten. It was just too hard to stay angry around Josh. The little imp knew it, too.

The twenty-minute trip flew by as Joseph and Josh entertained themselves with some weird, made-up game that the guys played with Josh. Isaiah didn't pretend to understand the rules, or even the point of the game, but it seemed to provide no end of amusement for them. He looked over occasionally when the pair would break out into uncontrollable laughter, but he spent most of the time absorbed in his own thoughts. All too soon, they passed the sign for Edmonton.

"Feed store first," Isaiah announced. "Hopefully we can find everything there. If not, we might have to trek over to the Farm and Fleet in Barton."

"Should just go there first," Joseph muttered.

"Don't be such a pessimist," Isaiah countered.

"It's only an extra fifteen minutes," Joseph argued. "There's better stores. And Josh and I could get ice cream."

Isaiah raised an eyebrow and stared pointedly out of the windshield, where large flakes of snow were spitting down intermittently. "If you really want ice cream in this weather, be my guest," he said dryly. "The Dairy Queen in Edmonton is open year-round now."

Joseph grumbled something and slumped in his seat, folding his arms over his chest. Isaiah figured it was better for Joseph that he wasn't able to make out the words.

Josh watched the interchange with a furrowed brow. When he caught Isaiah's eye, he cocked his head in question.

"Nothing to worry about, squirt," Isaiah assured him. "Joseph is just a little cranky today."

"Cranky?"

Josh giggled. The word might have expressed disbelief, but Joseph's tone was, well, cranky.

Isaiah pulled to a stop in front of the feed store still chuckling. Josh was out the door before he even got the engine turned off, with Joseph hot on his heels.

Sometimes Isaiah wondered which one was the kid and which one the adult. Of course, he had the same thoughts about most of his guys—had done even before Josh came. Tommy, in particular, had a talent for bringing out the immature side of people.

Isaiah sauntered inside, giving Carl a brief wave. "Jameson," he called to the clerk. "I'm gonna need some feed. We went through the last batch quicker than expected. Price the same?"

"Went up thirty cents," Jameson called back. "I'll ring ya up and get Curtis ready to load."

Isaiah nodded his appreciation, heading for the tack. He passed Josh on the way and knocked the kid's hat askew. Josh grinned up at him.

"It ought not to be allowed."

The unfamiliar female voice was almost shockingly venomous. Isaiah's head swung around. A middle-aged blonde wearing the local uniform of boots and jeans stood a few feet away, glaring at him. When he caught her gaze, she took a step closer.

"You should be ashamed of yourself," she spat. "Exposing a child to your filth."

Isaiah took an involuntary step backwards, then stopped, not about to retreat from this. "Better my filth than your narrow-minded bigotry," he retorted.

Then he nearly smacked a hand over his mouth. *Stupid, Isaiah, really stupid. You know that only encourages them.*

"You just wait," she threatened. "When people find out what you're doing with that kid, someone will step in."

"What I'm doing?" Oh, hell, no. Now that was just uncalled for. "I'm raising my brother. Exactly what do you think is going on?"

His voice must have risen, because suddenly Joseph was there, laying a restraining hand on his arm.

"Come on, boss," Joseph urged. "We've got feed to load."

"Where's Josh?" Isaiah asked without taking his eyes off the woman.

"Carl took him outside. Come on, man. We've got work to do."

With one last glare, Isaiah spun around and let Joseph usher him outside. Once there, he planted his hands on his hips. Looking up, Isaiah stared blankly at the grey sky and let out a deep breath.

"Don't let it get to you," Joseph said in a low, intense voice. "She's just an old harpy. Don't pay any attention to her. Those who know you know you're not hurting anybody."

"You know how people are around here," Isaiah argued, sneaking a quick look to make sure Josh wasn't in earshot. "If they start stirring up trouble—"

"Don't go creating problems," Joseph advised. "He's your brother. You're his legal guardian. Not much anyone can do, huh?"

"I wouldn't bet on it. He's only my half-brother, and there's other family members out there. Just 'cause his mom thought I'd be best doesn't mean others would agree."

"Maybe you should lay low for a while, then," Joseph suggested. "Let people forget."

"You really think that will fix this?" Isaiah demanded. "Somehow I doubt me hiding is going to make any difference to the stiff-necked, backward, homophobic—"

Joseph cut his rant off with a quick hand motion and a nod of his head. Isaiah closed his eyes and took a few more breaths, trying to get his temper under control. His smile was probably a bit fake but it was the best he could do.

"Hey, Josh. Carl spoiling you?"

Josh tilted his head, eyes solemn. Goddamn it, the kid was too smart for his own good. Or at least, for Isaiah's peace of mind.

Isaiah's smile was more genuine this time, although still a touch forced. He dropped a hand onto Josh's shoulder and squeezed.

"Come on, kiddo. You can help me load up. Then maybe you and Joseph can get that ice cream he was talking about."

"Boss…"

Isaiah shook his head. "You've got the list," he said softly over his shoulder. "I'm not going back in. Best if I work off some of my temper, huh?"

Joseph nodded his agreement, face still set in worried lines. Isaiah didn't feel like soothing him, though. Hell, there really wasn't anything to say that would do the trick, anyway. The situation was what it was. Hopefully, most people were too smart to listen to the rumours.

Isaiah kept one hand on Josh, though, as they wandered towards Carl, who was watching them with concern and questions in his bright eyes. Another head shake forestalled any questions.

Isaiah didn't really hold out much hope on that whole 'too-smart' thing. Because in general? People in groups tended to be really quite stupid. Gullible. Vicious.

The best thing to do right now was pretend he didn't see it, protect Josh as well as he could, and get on with his life.

* * * *

Grady stepped out into the cool night air, zipping his coat and turning up the sheepskin collar. The sound of footsteps rapidly heading his way made him turn. Past the dim glow cast by the streetlight, three familiar, bulky forms emerged.

Grady cursed low and viciously. He really didn't want to deal with this. Not ever, and certainly not tonight. But there was no avoiding the inevitable. Ever since the rumours had started circulating again. It was, in fact, partly what urged him into town tonight—best to deal with the problem in the usual way and then let the whole thing blow over.

Ever since Isaiah had told Grady what had happened in town earlier, Grady had been bracing himself for this. He'd dreaded it all afternoon. Now, he just wanted it over.

Grady turned as the three men, the banes of his existence, gathered around him.

"Well, well," one drawled. "If it isn't the village idiot."

Grady scowled. "I've really got better things to do than stand here and listen to your bullshit."

"Not nice, Grady, not nice at all." Torres had mean, squinty little eyes that had only gained a stronger, nastier light as he had grown older. Time did not, unfortunately, work for all bullies. Some men remained bullies. Also unfortunately, time did give them bigger muscles and stronger fists.

Of course, time had done the same for Grady, too.

Morris leaned against the lamppost, puffing lazily on his cigarette. Grady kept a close eye on the smallest of the three men. Despite his wiry frame, Morris was the most dangerous, and the most likely to start trouble.

Morris took another drag, blowing out a stream of smoke. When he spoke, his voice was casual, nonchalant. It didn't fool Grady for a second.

"Word on the street is your boy was seen coming out of that bar again."

Grady grunted. "Word on the street is more often wrong than not."

"Yeah, but that's the third time in six months. What did we tell you last time?"

Grady kept his mouth clamped shut in a stubborn line.

Thomason bumped him on the shoulder. Grady staggered sideways a few steps, ignoring the mocking laughter out of pure habit.

Thomason laughed harder than the rest. The sound had a mean edge to it, and Grady switched his focus. The big mechanic would be the one to start things tonight, then.

He was proven right. He saw the fist fly through his peripheral vision right before it slammed into his jaw. Grady grunted as pain shot through his face and his head snapped back from the force of the blow.

Morris flicked his cigarette aside and the trio closed in. All mocking was gone now — their faces serious and hard.

"We've told you more than once to get rid of that fag foreman of yours," he snarled. "Guess we're just gonna have to remind you again."

Grady let them herd him away from the streetlight and into the narrow alley between the dark drugstore and the equally dark law firm. He wanted to draw attention even less than they did. It always ended up with him in a cell and the trio graciously, after much dithering, agreeing not to press charges.

Grady waited until the shadows closed around them before wading in. His fist landed against flesh and he got in more good licks than usual before the first blow to the stomach left him gasping for air.

After that, it was the usual slaughter that occurred when one guy faced three opponents.

* * * *

Isaiah shoved open the door, already knowing what he was going to find. When Grady didn't show up at the barn at his usual time, there were only a couple of possibilities. The most likely was what Isaiah found in the office.

Grady was sprawled on the couch, one muscular forearm slung over his eyes. His hair stuck up every which way, clothes messy and covered in dirt and stains.

Isaiah sighed and headed straight for the kitchen. Unable to find any of the ice packs he'd bought a few weeks ago, he dug out a plastic bag and filled it with ice cubes. Next he filled a glass of water then grabbed the bottle of aspirin.

It was a familiar, if hated, ritual. Grady was normally growly but hard to provoke. Except every month or so, he'd go into town, tie one on, and pick a fight.

Isaiah consoled himself with the thought that at least this time he hadn't needed to go bail the man's ass out of jail.

Isaiah headed back to the office and sat down on the sturdy pine coffee table, holding out the bag of ice. Grady didn't look at him, just stuck his hand out and took the offering. Grady lifted his arm enough to plop the makeshift icepack on his black eye but didn't stir any further.

"Any fines I need to take care of?" Isaiah asked quietly.

Grady shook his head.

Isaiah sighed, letting the silence grow until it became uncomfortable. Grady held out his hand and Isaiah moved on to the next step, passing over two white pills. Grady finally sat up, swallowing the aspirin with the glass of water. Grady's eyes weren't quite as blood-shot as normal, but that didn't mean much. Unlike Isaiah, who wandered around in a fog for a solid twelve hours after an alcohol binge, Grady didn't really feel the hangover effects the next morning. Just the effects from whatever fight he'd wandered into.

"Ready to talk now?"

Grady grimaced.

Isaiah sighed again. "Grady, you really have to stop doing this. One day you're going to throw a punch at the wrong person and the judge will lock you up and throw away the key."

Grady glared through narrowed eyes. Isaiah slid back on the table a couple of inches, surprised at the reaction.

"What makes you think I start anything?" Grady snapped. His voice was low and rusty and he winced as speaking broke open his split lip. Isaiah handed him a tissue mechanically and gave a glare of his own.

"Because even the local yokels aren't dumb enough to pick a fight with a guy as huge as you are," Isaiah snapped back.

Grady gave a low chuckle, the sound completely devoid of mirth. "You'd be surprised."

A thud on the stairs had them both looking towards the hallway. Grady's eyes widened. Or at least, the eye not swollen shut.

Isaiah grunted. "Get your ass upstairs and cleaned up before Josh sees. The last thing I want to do is explain your condition to a ten-year-old."

Isaiah shoved himself to his feet and went to intercept his little brother. And pretended that he didn't see the hurt in Grady's normally emotionless hazel eyes.

Grady dragged himself up the stairs, feeling like he was trying to hike up a mountain. Each step jarred the bruises painfully. His eye might be the most visible, but it was actually the least bothersome. His back throbbed, low down, and Grady had the feeling he'd be pissing blood for the next couple of days. It wouldn't be the first time. Probably not the last, either.

The thought depressed him. He wanted to climb into bed, pull the covers up, and refuse to come out for the next month or so.

Instead, he headed for the master bathroom, stripping off his clothes as he crossed the bedroom. He left them littering the dark grey carpet like fallen leaves, not even wanting to think about picking up after himself. That would involve bending over. The thought was just too painful to contemplate at the moment.

Grady gave the shower a minute to warm up and stepped under the spray, groaning out loud when the hot water began to pound at the knots in his shoulders. He braced his arms on the cold tile, dropped his head forward and let the heat stream over his naked flesh. Little stings rippled his skin, cuts making themselves known for the first time. Damn, but it had been a while since they'd worked him over this badly.

Better him than Isaiah, though. Grady was…well— as sad as it was to admit—he was used to it. The taunts and the abuse. Isaiah had been, for lack of a better word, sheltered growing up. Oh, from stories he'd told, Isaiah hadn't managed to completely evade all the bigots. No gay man truly could, not without staying buried deep in the back of the closet. But the man had grown up in California. The Preston family had money and connections. Whereas Grady had grown up on this same ranch, with a father who believed in stern discipline. Not unlike many other fathers in the area. The rather one-sided battle between Grady and several of the local bullies had been ongoing for darn near two decades. And they weren't even one hundred per cent sure that Grady was gay.

He was, but he never came out and said it. Grady dealt with enough flack as it was for his stupidity and his choice of employees. Although if it wasn't the latter, it would be something else.

It had started clear back in grade school, when it became obvious that Grady wasn't like the other kids. Reading and writing hadn't just come with difficulty for him, it hadn't come at all. He'd dropped out in middle school and no one had ever seemed to care too much about getting him to go back. Especially his father.

Grady had tried to do better by Tracy, ensuring she not only finished high school but also went to college. Of course, so far her goal in life appeared to be seeing how much alcohol she could drink every night and how many parties she could attend before the sun rose. And occasionally after, as well. Grady figured it was out of his hands now. He sent money every so often — she was his sister, after all, and he couldn't let her go completely under. It just made him more and more jealous of Isaiah and Josh. The bond between them was so strong, and they were only half-brothers. What Grady wouldn't give to have someone in his life. Someone who belonged just to him. Hell, he'd even settle for sharing. Just as long as he had *someone* in his life who gave a shit.

And he wanted that someone to be Isaiah. He'd always wanted that, ever since the lanky man had shown up on his ranch all those years ago. Green and wet behind the ears, with a shiny new diploma and enough enthusiasm for three people, the man had tugged at Grady's heart from the very first. Now with Josh in the mix, Grady wanted to belong so badly he could almost taste it.

He remembered when Tracy had been that little, back before she'd learnt to hate him. God, he'd loved having a kid around. Some of them just had that knack of brightening the world around them. Tracy had, once. Josh did now. Life on a ranch could be difficult, dangerous, each day filled with more tasks than could be completed. It was so easy to get bogged down in the daily grind without someone to remind you that life could be fun, too. It was one of the reasons Grady had hired Tommy. The man had such a cheerful outlook, sometimes too much so, at least according to Joseph. That, and the fact that his sexual orientation had become common knowledge. It often wasn't safe on the rodeo circuit for a gay cowboy. When Grady had offered Tommy a job after the bull rider had been injured, Tommy hadn't even needed to think about it before accepting.

Grady shut off the water with a near savage motion. This round and round whirl of thoughts wasn't helping anyone, him least of all. It was time to go find something else to occupy himself with.

What Grady really wanted was to sleep, he thought, as he towelled his hair dry. But he knew himself well. If he tried right now, the thoughts would just continue to circle and he'd end up staring at the ceiling.

A quick swipe of the towel over his dripping skin and Grady yanked on jeans and a flannel shirt. He'd head out to the stable and try to find something to do. The horses soothed him when nothing else could.

And try to keep out of sight of Tommy and Josh. Isaiah had seen him already and Micah and Joseph would just shake their heads. But Tommy and Josh would take one look at his bruises and the cut on his cheekbone, now covered with a cartoon Band-Aid, and start in with the questions. Grady simply wasn't up to an interrogation right now. He just wanted to bury himself in the familiar work routine and be alone to lick his wounds.

Chapter Fourteen

Josh swung his sneaker-clad feet back and forth, banging against the fence with each pass. From his perch on the top corral post, he had a good view of the whole yard. School was out for the weekend, his backpack abandoned in the grass. He should be excited—after all Tommy had promised him a trail ride tomorrow, and possibly a camp out. At the very least, there would be hotdogs and marshmallows.

Instead, he sat out here, trying to come up with reasons *not* to go inside.

Things were getting tense, the air in his new house crackling with anger and unspoken words. Josh was all too familiar with the situation. He hated it. It was like that summer he'd spent with his mom and his last stepdad, the one who was always angry and ended up moving to France or something.

When his mother had died, not much had changed for Josh. At least, not at first. Then Isaiah had swooped in, the big brother he had dreamt of meeting for so long. It had been everything he'd hoped for and more.

His whole life had got turned upside down and it was great. Well, not his mom dying, but really, it was hard to be all that upset about someone he'd only seen, like, three times. But then Isaiah had brought him here, and Josh had met Grady, and he'd thought...

Well, it didn't really matter what he thought anymore, did it? Grady had been weird lately and Isaiah had been snappy and now they weren't talking or looking at each other or even sharing space. One would come in the room and the other would leave.

Josh's stomach rumbled and he patted it, telling it to hush. Dinner used to be something to look forward to, Grady and Isaiah swapping jokes and smiles, teasing him and each other. But the last two nights Grady would put the food out and disappear. Isaiah would shovel his own meal down, silent and...Josh had finally broken down yesterday and asked if Isaiah was angry at him. Isaiah just shook his head and told him to eat his food—that it wasn't anything to worry about.

But Josh *was* worried. He'd been building a perfect little life here and now it was getting all screwed up. He knew it had something to do with that lady at the feed store. He understood that she was angry at Isaiah because he didn't like girls. Isaiah had explained all about it. Josh really couldn't see why his brother's dating habits mattered to some strange lady that he'd never met.

Josh jerked his head up when the screen door slammed. Grady came stomping down the front steps of the house, hands shoved deep in his pockets, eyes glued to the dirt. He looked sad.

Josh lifted his hand to wave, then paused mid-motion. Grady was dragging his feet, walking to his truck, but it was the expression on his face that stopped Josh from hailing him. He looked kind of how Josh felt before school on test days. Like he was going to have to do something that he really didn't want to do.

Josh hunkered down as best he could without moving, watching as Grady climbed into his truck. Then the big rancher just sat there for a minute—hands on the wheel, staring at nothing. Even from here, Josh could see him heave a sigh before the engine roared to life.

The truck pulled away, leaving a thick cloud of dust hanging in the air. Josh chewed on his thumbnail and thought hard, studying the trail left behind by Grady's departure. Wherever Grady was going, Josh could tell he hadn't wanted to. Josh would go get Tommy—he would be the most likely to listen, to help—but Tommy was a couple of miles out doing...something. Josh still didn't understand what exactly the cowboys did all day, when they rode out into the tree-covered wilderness and wandered the miles of grassy plains.

It took Josh nearly five minutes, but he finally reached a conclusion. This had gone on long enough. Grady wasn't happy and needed someone to help him. Isaiah wasn't happy and needed to get the stick out of his butt. They were both being stupid.

So it was, apparently, up to Josh to fix things. This was his family, Grady and Isaiah and the guys, and he was going to fight for it. He'd never had a family before. His mother didn't count. She'd always been distant and far more concerned with her life than with him. But this, here, on the ranch, this was the family he'd always wanted and it was worth fighting for, worth trying to keep in one piece.

Josh hopped off the fence, stumbling a bit when his feet hit the uneven ground. He took a few steps, backtracked and snatched up his backpack, then took off, slinging the bag over his shoulder. Around this time of day, Isaiah was usually in one of the two breeding barns, brushing out one of his beloved mares.

He tramped past the bright red main barn, the low sounds of whickering floating out from the horses not being used today. Small paddocks butted up to each stall, with doors leading out to give the animals fresh air and more room. He circled around the side, patting a few big heads as he passed. Then it was down the hill and up to the first of the two smaller barns, nestled in a little dip side-by-side.

"That's a girl, so lovely, yes." The sound of his brother's voice from inside told Josh he'd guessed correctly. He dumped his bag at the door and entered carefully, giving his eyes a few moments to adjust to the dim light.

Isaiah was at the end of the long, wide centre aisle, grooming a pretty little bay mare.

"Hey, kiddo," Isaiah called, quietly so as not to startle the obviously skittish horse. "Good day at school?"

Josh shrugged, stopping near the mare's — Ashley's — head and stroked her flank.

"Need something?" Isaiah asked absently. He rubbed the currycomb along Ashley's hindquarters, glancing up over her back to meet Josh's stare.

Josh nodded. Isaiah paused in his motions, cocking his head expectantly.

It was times like these that Josh felt his lack keenly. If he could *tell* Isaiah, let his tone of voice convey his worry...but it wasn't possible and Josh had long ago accepted that. It was what it was.

"Grady went to town," he signed.

"So?"

"You need to go get him."

"Grady's a big boy, he can handle himself." Isaiah's tone was cranky, the words final, and he went back to his work like Josh hadn't spoken.

Josh wanted to throw back his head and scream. Loudly. But that wasn't fair to Ashley. She'd freak and it wasn't her fault that Josh's brother was being a big doofus.

"I think he needs help."

It took Josh waving wildly to get Isaiah's attention. Isaiah sighed.

"Josh, I know you like Grady, but what he does in his free time is really none of our business. Now, why don't you go up to the house and get a snack? I'll be up soon."

Josh shook his head violently and stamped his foot. *"I mean it. Grady needs help. You need to go find him."*

Isaiah sighed again and rested his arms on top of Ashley's back, brush dangling. "All right, I can see you aren't gonna let this go. What makes you say he needs help?"

"He didn't want to go. He looked upset and people in town are being mean right now and – "

Isaiah cut off Josh's frantic motions with a quick wave of his brush. "Josh—"

"Don't." Josh put all the disgust he was feeling into the abrupt movements of his signing. Disappointment churned in his stomach. He glared fiercely at his brother, equal parts furious at Isaiah and at himself for the tears he felt burning in his eyes. He couldn't really explain why he was so upset, why he *knew* it was important for Isaiah to go after Grady. He just *did.*

But, like so many times before, he couldn't figure out how to make his feelings clear. Josh sniffed and turned to leave.

"Josh."

Josh paused but didn't turn, not willing to look at his brother and risk looking like a big baby when he started to cry.

"It's really that important to you?" Isaiah asked quietly.

Josh nodded. *"He needs to be here for dinner,"* he half-turned to tell Isaiah. *"He hasn't been in days and I want him here. Like a family again."*

A long pause dragged through the barn, interspersed by shifting bodies and low snorts from the other horses in the stalls, the sounds familiar and normally, comforting. Finally, boots scraped on concrete then two big hands settled on his shoulders.

"All right," Isaiah conceded. "I'll go find Grady."

Josh turned and flung himself at his brother, wrapping his arms around Isaiah's waist and squeezing with all his might. Isaiah chuckled.

"Little brat."

One of these days Isaiah was going to have to learn to say no to Josh. Otherwise, the kid was going to work him over good, especially once they hit those teenage years. But, as always, Josh put on that miserable face and sort of hunched into himself and Isaiah caved.

Which was how he found himself parking his truck on Main Street, pissed off and annoyed, but resolved to track down his boss. Who probably didn't want to be tracked down — they would have another argument and... He slammed the truck door and stomped across the parking lot, not sure if he was more angry or frustrated. Whatever he was, the maelstrom of emotions was making his gut churn.

Isaiah's deep scowl made more than one person move swiftly out of his way. He shoved open the door to D'Arcy's, scowling fiercely at the smoky interior. Dim lights only enhanced the haze hovering over the crowd of cowboys, farmers and assorted patrons all busy celebrating Friday night.

The door smacked him in the butt, knocking him off-balance and sending him staggering across the floor where he nearly took out a huge dude in biker leathers. Isaiah decided he'd be better off doing his searching from a corner, not right in front of the door. He stepped to one side, eyes narrowed as he scanned the bar.

"Can I help you with something, handsome?"

Isaiah barely spared the lush blonde a second look. "Not tonight, honey. I'm not here to have fun."

"Didn't think anyone came in here for any other reason."

"I'm looking for someone," Isaiah explained. "Tall, broad-shouldered, dark hair and eyes? Dillon Grady?"

"Oh, Grady." She sniffed. He couldn't tell if she didn't like Grady, or if she'd just got a bit too much smoke up her nose. "He hasn't been here in a good six, eight months. Smart of him, you ask me."

Six or...no, it would most likely have been about eight months ago. That was the last time Isaiah had been called down to haul Grady out of jail. His boss had slugged some local cowhand for reasons unknown and ended up cooling his heels in the sheriff's office for the next four hours until Isaiah could come bail him out.

But if Grady hadn't been into D'Arcy's since then, where the hell was he going?

"Thanks, honey," Isaiah said absently. He thought briefly about fortifying himself with a quick drink, but then decided he didn't want to waste the time trying to plough his way through the crowd to the bar. Most people would think D'Arcy's was the only bar in town, instead of one of five. It was by far the most popular, although for the life of him, Isaiah couldn't see why. He far preferred a little out-of-the-way place with a room you could actually walk across, a crowd that consisted of at least a few people who didn't chain-smoke, and music that you could decipher instead of stuff turned up so loud all it did was shake the floor over the roar of the crowd.

Isaiah beat a hasty retreat — or at least, as hasty as you could get in that place. He burst out onto the street. Once he got a bit of distance from the front door, he inhaled a deep breath of clear air.

The edge was gone off the anger that had sustained him clear to town. He still wasn't a very happy cowboy, but he wasn't ready to tear Grady's head off this time. Irritated, yes. Punch-first-ask-questions-later mad, no.

He shoved his hands into his pockets and headed down the sidewalk in the direction of the next bar. Now that his ire had cooled, Isaiah could admit that it had been more hurt than anything. *Here I'd thought that having me and Josh would maybe...*

The sun was dipping back down behind the low buildings. Isaiah's stomach growled menacingly, reminding him that he'd been too mad to eat. He'd left the boys in charge of Josh. They'd probably end up microwaving hotdogs or something for dinner, but Isaiah figured it wouldn't hurt this once. He'd never cared about eating healthy until Josh came around. Now the thought of some of the crap he and the boys used to scarf down made him nauseous. Life was funny sometimes — funny strange, not funny ha-ha. Though with Tommy around, it was often both. At the same time.

Twenty minutes later, Isaiah stepped inside the third bar on his list. His earlier irritation was starting to rear up again, anger right on its heels. If he didn't find Grady soon, his stomach was going to gnaw its way free in search of food. Isaiah had far better things to do than tramp all over Edmonton looking for his wayward boss, but damned if he wanted to explain to Josh why Grady wasn't there to watch cartoons with him tonight, as they'd been in the habit of doing on weekends. Grady could play the jerk all he wanted to Isaiah, but Isaiah sure as hell wasn't going to let Grady disappoint Josh.

Isaiah finally got lucky. In the last bar he tried. Figured.

"Yeah, Grady was here earlier. Had a beer then headed for the back. Probably went out to have a smoke."

Grady didn't smoke, but Isaiah didn't bother taking the time to explain that to the bored bartender. Boots ringing on the scarred wooden floor, Isaiah headed to the back of the small building. He followed the small hallway past the restrooms and to the back door, propped open to air the close confines out a bit. Isaiah pushed the door open and stepped outside.

Right into a flying fist. The punch caught him in the jaw and Isaiah stumbled backward, ears ringing. A roar filled his ears and he shook his head to clear it.

Isaiah looked up and got a good look at the action. Oh, hell no. That was just not fair.

His anger burst free again, although this time it had a new target. Namely, the three guys pinning Grady against a wall. Grady was giving it his best, but his nose was bleeding and he was hunched a bit over his stomach.

Isaiah stalked up behind the nearest man and tapped him on the shoulder.

"Butt out." The man turned around to snarl at the interruption and Isaiah let him have it. His fist connected with a solid, satisfying thunk.

"Isaiah, get out of here."

"Shut up, Grady."

Isaiah swung out and landed a good kick at the man he'd just slugged, immensely pleased when the man hit the ground. The other two stared at him for a minute, frozen in obvious shock that anyone would interfere.

Then the smallest of them — Isaiah thought the bastard's name was Clinton Morris — shook off his surprise.

"This is none of your business, fag," he snapped. "We're dealing with the idiot right now. We'll get to you later."

"You did *not* just say that." Isaiah donned his best snarl and dived at the man. They slammed together and hit the ground, rolling. Behind and above them, Grady yelled something. Over the panting breath in his ear, Isaiah heard the sound of smacking flesh. He sure hoped it was Grady doing the hitting, because he was too occupied at the moment to help his boss out.

Isaiah blocked a knee that would have done significant damage to one of his best features and elbowed Morris in the gut. Hard. The smaller man gagged in his ear and Isaiah rolled aside just in time, as Morris vomited onto the cement.

Two down, one to go. Isaiah stood up, brushing himself off. Nope, none to go. While he'd been preoccupied, Grady had apparently pulled himself together long enough to slam the third man into the nearest wall. He now lay sprawled at Grady's feet, mouth gaping as he lay unconscious in a pile of dirty snow.

Isaiah leaned over and braced his hands on his knees, trying to catch his breath. Now that the danger was over and the adrenaline rush was beginning to dissipate, his jaw stung like a son of a bitch.

"Isaiah, what the fuck are you doing here?" Grady leaned against a wall, looking not much better than Isaiah felt.

"Looking for you, what else? Want to explain what the hell I just walked into?"

Grady shrugged. "Just the usual."

Something about Grady's words rang false. Or at least, false with the usual story he fed Isaiah. For one thing, Grady looked stone-cold sober. Getting jumped—because that was clearly what had happened—was generally enough to start the process. But Grady didn't look like he'd been drinking much and when Isaiah leaned closer, all he could smell was blood and the faintest hint of beer.

Isaiah straightened and yanked his shirt out of his jeans, using the edge to wipe some of the sweat off his face. Didn't matter how cold it was, fighting worked up a sweat.

"Come on," he said evenly. "Let's get out of here before they come around. I've got some rags in the truck. You can clean yourself up and we'll get something to eat. You can tell me all about your little Friday night adventures over food."

Chapter Fifteen

Isaiah exited the small alley, slipping on a patch of ice. Grady grabbed him, but the man was none too steady himself and nearly took them both down.

"Do me a favour," Isaiah said. "Don't help."

"Sorry."

Isaiah couldn't seem to find his anger anymore. Of course, nothing relieved stress quite like a good old-fashioned knock-down, drag-out fight. But beyond that, Grady looked so miserable. Isaiah had seen that same chastised look on Josh's face a few days ago, when he'd been caught sneaking out to the barn at two in the morning. Isaiah thought sometimes they might as well just build the kid a bedroom in the stable and stop fighting upstream.

Streetlights were flickering on all down the street as they reached Isaiah's truck. He unlocked it and rooted in the back, coming up with a couple of extremely stained towels. They'd do the job. He chucked one at Grady. Grady didn't duck fast enough and caught the towel right in the face. Isaiah had to snicker a bit at that.

Grady peeled the towel from his face and wiped at his nose.

"Here, let me do that," Isaiah said. "You're just smearing."

Grady's hand dropped to one side as Isaiah used a second towel to wipe away the worst of the blood streaking Grady's sharp features.

"Well, it's not broken," Isaiah commented when he finally removed enough blood to examine Grady's nose. "That's something at least."

"Sure feels broken," Grady groused.

"Yeah, I'm sure it does. Your eyes are gonna be beautiful tomorrow."

"Great."

Something in Grady's eyes made Isaiah suddenly uncomfortable. He finished cleaning up the most visible injuries, swiped at his knuckles, and tossed the towels back into the truck.

"Come on," he ordered in a hoarse voice that really didn't sound like his. "I was starving before that fight. Now I'm about ready to pass out."

"So that's where Josh gets it," Grady commented.

"Gets what?"

"That incredible appetite that belongs on someone about three times your size."

"Oh. That." Isaiah shrugged. "It's been a long day and I didn't get lunch."

They climbed into the truck and Isaiah pointed his ancient baby in the direction of his favourite restaurant. They made the drive in a silence that was surprisingly not awkward. Normally Isaiah would be wiggling in his seat with the need to get answers, but not this time. He figured it was probably because he halfway knew what sort of explanation he'd be getting. And he didn't really want to hear it.

But he needed to.

Isaiah pulled up in front of the small steakhouse, pleased when he was able to find a spot that didn't require parking three blocks away. The Lone Star was a popular place, but they were able to get right in. Once Isaiah had ordered a beer — and it didn't escape his notice that Grady ordered iced tea — he plopped his menu on the table, folded his hands on top of it, and stared at Grady with probing eyes. Isaiah was extremely pleased with himself when the man actually squirmed a touch on the bench. Isaiah had been practicing his stern expression. He figured it was the first parenting skill he should acquire.

"So," he drawled evenly. "You want to tell me what's going on?"

Grady drew small circles with the water that had dripped off his glass and onto the gleaming wood. "It's nothing," he hedged. "Just a couple of guys I don't get along with."

"It's a bit more than that and we both know it. Rib eye, medium rare, slaw and onion rings," he told the waiter. He didn't need to look at the menu. Isaiah wasn't ashamed to admit he was a creature of habit.

"Same," Grady said, handing over his menu. Isaiah waited for the server to leave before he pounced again.

"What I want to know is why you let me assume that you were coming into town and picking fights. Why the hell didn't you tell me you were getting jumped?"

"Are you so sure that's what happened every time? Maybe that's normally how it goes."

"Grady, you're testing my patience," Isaiah declared.

Grady sighed and looked away. His finger had stopped circling but now his knee was jiggling. Isaiah could feel it brushing against his leg. He wanted to reach over and hold Grady still but settled for bumping the other side of the booth with his heel.

"Grady."

Grady sighed again.

"You're gonna make me think you're asthmatic."

"You know, you're in a pretty good mood for someone who just got in a fight," Grady pointed out.

"I'm in a good mood *because* I just got in a fight," Isaiah corrected. "I've been edgy all day. Slugging that jerk made it all go away. Like magic. Maybe I'll have to join you in town more often."

"You don't want to do that."

Isaiah raised his eyebrows and slid back in his seat, crossing his arms over his chest. "We've got a good twenty minutes before the food gets here. Even then, I'm not moving until you start talking. So, start."

"I'm... Did you know I never finished high school?"

Okay. Not what he'd been expecting to hear, but Isaiah could run with it. "Hate to tell you, big guy, but that's not all that unusual around here."

"I dropped out of school in sixth grade."

But that *was* unusual. "They let you do that?"

Grady shrugged. "They were glad to be rid of me, to be honest. I was making them look bad."

"I don't see how. You were just a kid. What, did you make a habit of spray-painting bad words on the gym wall or something?"

"No," Grady replied. "That would have been Morris."

"Ah. The bastard I slugged earlier?"

"Yep."

"Excellent. I always like it when I actually punch out someone unlikeable."

"You are so strange sometimes."

"But I got you to smile, didn't I?"

Grady's lips went from twitching to full-out tilting. Damn, but the man looked good when he smiled. His hazel eyes lightened and the lines around the corners deepened. This time it was Isaiah who squirmed, but it sure as hell wasn't from nerves. No, sir. He was just trying to keep his suddenly constricting jeans from squashing something important.

"So, tell me about why you dropped out. And about Morris and his little buddies."

The smile slid away. Isaiah would have mourned its loss, but Grady didn't give him time.

"Morris, Thomason, and Ellis hate me. Always have, ever since we went to school together. But I..." Grady stopped and bit his lip. "I don't want you to change the way you look at me," he confessed.

"And how do I look at you?" Isaiah asked with genuine interest.

"Like I'm somebody special."

The words were whispered so quietly that Isaiah actually had to lean over the table a bit to hear them over the slight buzz of the crowded restaurant.

"Grady, you are someone special." He should have felt like a dork saying that, but instead it felt...right. Grady was a far better man than he seemed to think and he held a very important place in Isaiah's life. Maybe it was time Isaiah showed him.

"Why did you drop out of school so young?" Isaiah pressed. Somehow, this was at the heart of everything, he knew it. The distance Grady kept between himself and others, the low opinion he had of himself. And most especially the way he didn't seem to think he was good enough for Isaiah.

"I can't read," Grady confessed.

"All right," Isaiah said slowly. "So your reading level is a little underage. We can work on—"

"No, I *can't* read," Grady insisted. "I never could. When the other kids were all learning how to string letters together into words and sentences, I just looked at a page full of weird symbols that I could never decipher, no matter how desperately I tried."

"You're dyslexic." Isaiah didn't know why he was surprised, really. It made a heck of a lot of sense. The way Grady had been so desperate to find a new business manager that he'd hire a greenhorn right out of college. The way he always assisted Isaiah with the books—mainly by tossing ideas around from opposite sides of the room. The way he signed his name, just two big scrawls where the only letters identifiable were the 'D' and the 'G'.

"Grady, a learning disability isn't anything to be ashamed of," Isaiah said earnestly. "I don't think less of you. Hell, I think I probably admire you even more. To be where you are, you must have fought damn hard."

"You know why the books were such a mess when you took the job?" Grady's jaw was clenched and he spat the words out.

Isaiah gave a sigh of his own and sat back. For some reason, Grady seemed determined to make Isaiah think badly of him. It wasn't going to happen, but Isaiah would let Grady vent for a bit before Isaiah told him that. "The books were pretty screwed up," Isaiah said by way of encouragement.

"After my dad died, my sister Tracy took over handling the business side of the ranch. She let the whole system go to hell because all she cared about was milking as much cash as she could out of the accounts. You know what she said the day she left? That it was easy because I was too much of an idiot to figure out what was going on."

"Sorry to say this, but your sister sounds like a real bitch."

"She is. But she was right."

Isaiah had a flashback to the fight and the word Morris had sneered. *Idiot.*

"You're not an idiot," Isaiah told Grady firmly. "In fact, I think you're probably one of the smartest guys I've ever known. You can't read, but you've done a pretty darn amazing job of coming up with creative ways to cope with that lack. A guy lacking in the intelligence department wouldn't be able to do that."

Grady clearly wasn't buying it. All right, Isaiah wasn't giving up, but he'd shelve the topic for now. He let Grady have a few moments reprieve while he finished his beer. Then their food came and Isaiah remembered how hungry he was. When about half his steak was gone and his stomach had stopped snarling, he decided Grady's reprieve was over.

"Somehow I don't see Morris beating you up on a semi-monthly basis just because you can't read," he proposed. "So are you going to tell me exactly what those fights have been about?"

"I already told you, they hate me."

"Grady, you can't lie worth a damn. Never play poker with Josh."

Grady snorted, choking on his tea. "That's a new one."

"Yeah. The boys decided to educate him. I think they're regretting it now."

"They know about you."

Isaiah put down his glass, taken by surprise when Grady blurted out the words so quickly that they tumbled practically on top of each other.

"Know what?" he asked.

"That you're...you know, gay." Grady whispered the last word like a little old lady confessing a shameful secret to her preacher.

"Yeah, so? You got a problem with that?"

"Of course not." Grady scowled. "But, well, Morris and his bunch do. Have a problem with it, I mean."

"So what the hell does that have to do with you?"

As soon as the question left his lips, realisation struck Isaiah with about the same force as that earlier fist to his jaw.

"Oh, hell no," he spat. "You have not been taking beatings for me."

Grady's expression said it all.

"Damn it, Grady!" Isaiah's curse was loud enough to turn heads. He quickly lowered his voice, staring poisonous daggers at his boss. "I can take care of myself. I don't need you to defend me to those assholes."

"I didn't want you to get hurt." Grady's voice was far from forceful, the man obviously realising that any argument he made wasn't going to be enough.

Isaiah stood and dug his wallet out of his back pocket. He threw down some bills, not even interested in finishing off his onion rings. Grady's confession had killed off the last of his appetite.

"Let's go," he said flatly. "I don't think this is a conversation we want to continue in public."

"Probably not."

The whole way back to the ranch, Isaiah kept sneaking glances in his rear view mirror at the truck following him. He didn't trust Grady not to bolt off for parts unknown. The man had looked nervous as hell when they'd left the restaurant.

Well, that was just too damn bad. Isaiah was determined that they were going to have this whole damn mess out in the open before the night ended. They'd been dancing around too many issues—not the least of which was their mutual attraction—for far too long. Isaiah was fed up and he was going to finally grow a set and do something about it. Grady was obviously not going to make the first move, so it was up to Isaiah.

Isaiah was going to give the man what he wanted, give him the life he deserved, even if it half-killed him—Grady, that was. Isaiah had no doubts that he was going to come through this just fine.

He parked his truck in its usual spot next to the main barn. Grady drove past him and up to the house. The opening of the garage door spilled a stark square of light across the driveway. The yard was quiet and still. Josh must still be hanging out with the guys. Either that or he'd escaped Tommy to hide out with the horses. Either one was fine with Isaiah. He figured his fight might be easier without an audience. Not easy—Grady would see to that, the stubborn bastard—but easier.

Isaiah hopped out of the truck and strode up to the house, shrugging on his coat as he went. He'd stripped it off inside the warm exterior of the truck but the air outside was enough to whip right through his flannel shirt.

He waylaid Grady at the front steps. Grady made as if to walk right past Isaiah, but Isaiah grabbed his arm and swung him around.

"We aren't done yet," he said.

"Yes, we are." Grady's voice may have been cold, but his eyes weren't. Maybe it was just Isaiah's imagination, but it seemed like Grady was pleading with him, eyes dark with desperation. It seemed to Isaiah that the man was stuck in a prison of his own making. He figured it was up to him to find the key to that big-assed lock.

"No, we aren't," Isaiah countered. "You haven't told me yet why the hell you've been heading off to Edmonton, knowing you're going to get your ass kicked, without telling anyone or asking for any help. You don't have to go there and—"

"Yes, I do," Grady shouted. Isaiah would have felt more satisfaction at breaking the dam if Grady hadn't looked quite so tormented. "I don't want you to leave."

"Why the hell would I leave?" Isaiah asked, floundering about in complete confusion. Damn conversation was worse than a minefield. He never knew when he was going to trigger the next explosion.

Grady clamped his mouth shut.

"You don't get to make a claim like that and then not explain," Isaiah said, starting to get pissed off. Or, if truth were told, more pissed off. After this conversation, he might just have to go pick another fight to relieve his stress. Tommy was usually good for it, although the man packed a wallop that would leave his ears ringing for days.

Of course, Isaiah could think of another marvellous way to release stress, but his chances for dragging Grady into bed for some bone-melting sex weren't looking good.

"Look," Grady said. "As long as they have a target, they're happy. Don't care too much who it is, either. If

I keep them occupied, they won't spread the word around town, about your orientation."

Like he gave a shit about that. Everyone already knew.

"And yours?" Isaiah pointed out.

Grady didn't confirm it, but then he didn't deny it, either. Not like he needed to, in any case. Isaiah had known the man swung his way from the very first. He'd been looking carefully for proof and had found it in Grady's utter lack of interest in any female around. Even the pretty and overly willing ones.

"I didn't want word to get out," Grady insisted. "It wouldn't go over very well around here."

"Everybody already knows!"

"No, they suspect. It's different to *know*."

"You're not making any sense. Besides, it works fine for Marcy and Lilith," Isaiah pointed out.

"But they're girls," Grady countered. "And they live in Barton."

"Don't know what their gender has to do with anything, and we can just start doing our shopping in Barton," Isaiah snapped. "I can't see how you putting yourself into the line of fire every few weeks helps the situation."

"I had to protect you," Grady insisted.

Oh, the man's mind just made no sense whatsoever.

"I don't get you," Isaiah nearly growled in an echo of his thoughts.

"Yeah, well, join the club."

"You're being ridiculous!" Isaiah shouted. "What the hell do you want from me?"

Instead of answering, Grady lunged. He grabbed the back of Isaiah's head, tangling his fingers tightly in Isaiah's hair, as he crushed their mouths together. Isaiah froze in pure shock for a split second before instinct took over and he tilted his head, sucking Grady's tongue into his mouth. He wrapped his hands around those broad shoulders, pulling Grady's shorter, stockier body into his. They moaned together as the kiss burned hotter. Grady couldn't seem to pull his hands loose, although he kept tugging at the short strands of hair in his grasp. Isaiah ran his palms over the sleek muscles of Grady's back, down to his waist, caressing the skin above his ass through the thin cotton of his T-shirt.

Damn. Kissing Grady was everything he'd ever imagined and more. The man radiated heat like a wood stove, his mouth burning around Isaiah's tongue as Grady sucked and inspected. A deep groan rumbled up from Isaiah's chest.

At the sound, Grady yanked back. He stared at Isaiah with wide eyes, his face slowly draining of colour.

"Oh, God," he whispered. Then he turned tail and ran.

Chapter Sixteen

Isaiah stood, frozen, lost in a haze of lust. It took a second for him to realise that his man was actually running away from him.

"Oh, no, you don't," he snarled at the rapidly retreating figure. Unfortunately, it took Isaiah's body endless seconds to catch up with his brain, and for his throbbing erection to subside enough that he could give chase.

And give chase he did. Isaiah pounded around the side of the house and headed straight for the barns. He knew Grady, knew where the man was going. What the man was thinking? Not so much.

Luck was on Isaiah's side. Luck, and good friends. As he neared the first corral, Josh paused. He turned, hand still wrapped around the lead rope of his mare, and pointed to the south. Isaiah was halfway through the long aisle of the first stable when Tommy popped his head out of the tack room. For once, the big cowboy didn't have a ready quip. Like Josh, he just pointed.

By the time Isaiah finally reached the breeding barn, he'd stopped running. Now he was just stomping, irritation, fury, and hurt all vying for precedence. Large equine heads swung towards Isaiah as he entered, already hanging over the top half of their stall doors. All right, then. So someone had recently been here. The large double doors at the far end were tightly sealed and he hadn't been that far behind Grady. Fresh footprints in the sawdust, not yet covered up by large hooves, disappeared into the gloom.

Isaiah slammed the small side door closed, braced his feet apart, planted his hands on his hips, and threw back his head.

"Grady!" he bellowed. "Get your delectable ass out here right this minute!"

Silence. It grew, rubbing Isaiah's already rough nerves raw. He was just a hairsbreadth away from really losing his temper with Grady. This whole blasted drama had gone on long enough.

"Grady, you've got till the count of three," he shouted. His words echoed in the mostly empty barn. One of the horses whinnied loudly at him, as if to scold Isaiah for all his noise.

"I'm not a kid," Grady said softly.

Isaiah whirled and took a few steps until he could see into a nearby stall. It was one of the ones they used for storage, hay bales stacked along the sides nearly to the ceiling. Grady was sitting in the corner on top of a bale, arms wrapped around his legs. He looked like he was trying to make himself smaller, to melt into the compressed hay that formed his makeshift seat.

Isaiah let out a long breath, releasing most of his anger with it. Grady just looked so miserable huddling there, so unlike himself. His eyes were red, as if he was suppressing tears by sheer force of will. His face was still pale and his hands, where they were clenched around his calves, would probably be shaking if he didn't have his fingers wound so tightly together.

Isaiah stepped into the stall, blinking to adjust his eyes to the dim light. He ignored the way Grady stiffened and tried to pull even further into himself. Isaiah's mind raced for the proper words as he dropped down on the hay bale beside Grady.

"I'm sorry," Grady whispered before Isaiah could speak.

"For what?" Isaiah growled. Yeah, it was a stupid question, but in his defence, his mind wasn't really working at full speed just yet. His brain was still a good bit away, deep inside that kiss.

"I shouldn't have kissed you. It was wrong, and I'm sorry, and —"

"Shut up."

Grady's mouth closed with an audible snap. Isaiah ran a hand down his face, still trying to find the right words. He'd learnt something lately, something that he would never have imagined a few months ago. Grady was fragile. Not physically, but emotionally. His self-confidence was somewhere down around his boot heels. What Isaiah used to take for reserve, he now realised was a complete cluelessness about social interaction. The man simply didn't know how to relate to people, or how to get them to relate to him. It hardly helped that Grady had such a low opinion of himself that he always jumped to the worst conclusions.

"I'm not sorry." Isaiah decided it was past time to quit thinking and just dive in. "I've been wanting to do that for years now."

Grady stared at him, eyes wide in the dusty air.

Isaiah nearly had to sit on his hands to keep from reaching for Grady. "I'm a fool," he said fervently. When Grady started to protest, Isaiah rode right over him. "No, I am. For too long I've been going from one guy to another, never quite sure what it was that I was looking for, and never recognising it was right in front of me. I'll forever be grateful to Josh for that. When he came, I started thinking differently. Seeing things differently. It wasn't just me anymore, it was a family. For the last couple of years it's been impossible to picture my life without you somewhere around. After Josh, it became impossible to picture us, picture our small family, without you front and centre. Every time something happened, every time I started to panic over suddenly trying to raise a kid, the first thing I wanted to do was run to you. You're so good with Josh, so clear-headed when I get muddled. We've been a team for a long time. But it's not enough to be a team. I want us to be partners."

"I don't see the difference." Grady's voice was hoarse with some unnamed emotion. "I'm not going anywhere. You don't have to—"

"Would you stop it and *listen*?" Isaiah wanted to howl in frustration. Grady was a good listener, he truly was, but sometimes he just didn't *hear*. He had this weird world view that skewed everything beyond recognition. It made Isaiah alternately want to smack the man upside the head and squeeze him until they both ran out of breath.

Looking at Grady's closed-off face, his studiously blank eyes, Isaiah suddenly understood that words weren't going to work here. He could talk all night, but it wouldn't make a bit of difference in the end.

So he would have to act. Isaiah shrugged mentally and swallowed down a wicked grin. That was okay. Action was a hell of a lot more fun than talking, anyway.

Isaiah reached out and yanked Grady forward. Grady yelped, practically falling into Isaiah's lap. Isaiah kept a tight, almost painful grip on his soon-to-be lover, to keep the man from bolting again.

Then he dived down and sank into the kiss that had been preoccupying his subconscious ever since Grady had touched him earlier.

This time it was Grady who froze. He pushed at Isaiah's shoulders and struggled a bit. Isaiah ignored him. The attempt to escape was half-hearted, at best. If Grady really wanted loose, Isaiah would have let him go. But right now, Isaiah didn't think Grady really knew what he wanted. Isaiah did, though, and he was going to give it to him.

Isaiah threaded his fingers through Grady's thick hair and tugged his head to the side, deepening the angle of the kiss. After several endless, agonising seconds, Grady responded, tentatively at first, then with growing confidence. Isaiah pushed for entrance and Grady opened his mouth enough for Isaiah to gain entrance. With that little concession, Grady yielded. His whole body sagged, leaning heavily into Isaiah's. Grady wrapped his large hands around Isaiah, moving them up his back. Still, the touch was light, as if Grady expected to be pushed away any second.

Not going to happen. Isaiah fell into the most stirring kiss he'd ever been a part of. His cock was hard, arousal raging through his body, but it was a distant feeling. He was too busy savouring the feel of Grady in his arms, the connection between them as their lips moved and parted, hands teased and touched. Yeah, he wanted to throw Grady down and fuck him until they both passed out, but he would be just as content to sit there for the next week, losing himself in the kisses and caresses.

"Dillon," he moaned.

His lover pulled back in surprise. "What?"

Isaiah smiled, hand reaching out. He traced the familiar features with his fingers, running his thumb over swollen lips. "My Dillon," he said.

"You've never called me that before," Grady said softly. Honest to God, his smile was shy. Isaiah had never seen quite that emotion on his Grady. But it fit, the slightly flushed cheeks and the soft eyes looking far more natural on the man than that harsh, remote expression ever had.

Isaiah shrugged, knowing his smile was a little sad now, a little regretful. "I should have. You use 'Grady' like a shield to keep people at a distance, keep them from getting too close. But I won't let it work with me. Not anymore. You're my Dillon and have been for a very long time."

Grady tried to pull back. Isaiah tightened his grip and shook his head.

"Uh uh. Where do you think you're going?"

"I don't understand this. Any of it. What are we doing?"

"What we've both wanted for years."

"I've never… I mean, you never showed any interest. This is all really sudden and I just don't understand."

Isaiah sighed. Okay, so Grady was going to be stubborn again. Best to get it all out now. The man wouldn't enjoy the kisses — or anything further — until they finished talking.

"You're my boss," Isaiah pointed out. "And you keep everybody at a distance. When you interviewed me all those years ago I thought, no way in hell can I work for this man. I'll be walking around with a perpetual hard-on and I'll never be able to resist taking him to bed. But I took the job anyway and in less than a week you'd earned my respect and admiration. I couldn't treat you like all the other guys I took to bed and fucked. I respected you far too much for that. So I pushed any attraction aside, especially as you didn't seem to reciprocate."

"I've always wanted you," Grady admitted. "But you never showed any interest, either."

"Poor Dillon," Isaiah teased gently, rubbing at the deep lines of confusion in Grady's forehead. "You've gotten so good at hiding from everyone, even yourself. I owe Josh."

"Josh?"

"You softened after he came. And watching you with Josh...you looked at me the same way, did you know? Like my presence makes your world a little brighter place."

"That's nonsense," Grady protested. "My feelings for Josh aren't remotely like what I...feel for you."

"I know that." Isaiah resisted the urge to roll his eyes. "But the depth of caring is there for both of us. And seeing that, it made all those feelings I'd buried — but had never forgotten — surface. I want more from you. A lot more. So stop fighting and let me take you to bed."

Grady reared back. "What?"

"You're over-thinking this," Isaiah said. "Tommy can keep Josh occupied. Come inside with me. Let me show you that I'm not just fooling around. Let me show you what it can be like between us."

Grady took a deep breath, uncertainty flickering in his hazel eyes. "All right."

Isaiah had never heard two words that meant more in his life.

Grady followed Isaiah to the house, clinging tightly to his hand. This was a stupid idea, he berated himself. So stupid. They'd go upstairs and the sex would be the most fantastic in his life. Then Isaiah would come to his senses and leave and take Josh with him and where would Grady be?

But Isaiah had called him Dillon, another part of him argued. Isaiah had kissed him. Was even now still holding his hand as they crossed the yard, in full view of everyone.

"Stop fretting," Isaiah scolded gently. "And don't you dare talk yourself out of this."

Grady's grip on Isaiah tightened involuntarily. Talk himself out of it? No, no chance of that. He'd been waiting too long to have Isaiah. He wasn't going to back out now, no matter what might happen later.

"And now you're thinking too much."

Grady could almost hear the eye-roll in Isaiah's words as they went into the house.

"Sorry," Grady replied. "I can't help it."

"Well, maybe you can't, but I'm betting I can." Isaiah stopped them in their journey, pushing Grady up against the wall of the hallway and leaning in close, so very close. "I bet I can make you stop thinking entirely."

Grady moaned at the lean body pressing so tightly against his. "I know you can."

"So, less talk, more do. I've been waiting a hell of a long time for this and I'm through being patient."

Grady could get on board with that. They stepped into Grady's bedroom and Grady practically tackled Isaiah, sending them both tumbling onto the mattress. Isaiah's laugh rumbled through the room, the sensation sending a little thrill through Grady.

"Now who's impatient?"

"That would be me." Grady leaned over Isaiah, burying his nose in the crook of Isaiah's neck and inhaling deeply. Damn, but the man smelt good.

"I have to smell like crap," Isaiah grumbled. Grady thought it was damn cute, the slight tinge of red in the man's cheeks. "I've been rolling around in an alley and dumped on my ass twice today."

"You smell fantastic," Grady assured him with complete honesty. "Like you."

"And how does 'me' smell?" Isaiah teased.

"Familiar and arousing and…just amazing."

"Mmm. Good answer."

Isaiah rolled them until they lay side by side, pressed together from shoulder to ankle. Isaiah buried his hands in Grady's hair. He tilted Grady's head to one side and moved in. Grady melted under the kiss, muscles losing all their power under the touch he'd waited so long for. Isaiah's lips moved skilfully, teasing and seductive. His tongue sought entrance and Grady granted it eagerly. He sucked Isaiah's tongue into his mouth, a shiver racking his spine when Isaiah caressed the bumpy roof of his mouth.

"We could go take a shower," Isaiah murmured, lips lifting and pressing between words. "Together, of course."

"Later." Oh, yeah. Isaiah and water and soap, all slippery and gleaming. Hell yes, they would most definitely get to that later.

Grady slid his hands up under Isaiah's shirt, hands clutching at thick, well-defined muscles as Isaiah moved in for another kiss, each one hotter and more urgent than the one before. Grady groaned, wrapping one leg around Isaiah's thigh. His cock pressed against the zipper of his jeans, causing a sweet ache. Not enough to demand release, not quite yet, but more than enough to keep him strung out, on edge, and wanting more. Much more. Namely, everything Isaiah had to give him. And even that might not be enough in the end.

And he was trying to over think it again. Isaiah nipped him on the collarbone, the sting sharp even through fabric.

"Focus." Isaiah rose up onto one forearm. He slid the other hand along Grady's stomach and down to the bulge at his groin. Isaiah cupped him, squeezing with just enough force to wring a pleading moan from Grady.

"There it is," Isaiah said with a satisfied smile.

Two could play at that game. Grady bucked up and their hips mashed together. His aim was true as his trapped dick bumped into a counterpart in Isaiah's jeans.

"Oh, damn, babe," Isaiah gasped. "I think I need skin. Thirty seconds ago."

Their earlier exploration had been almost lazy, both of them savouring their long-delayed pairing. That feeling vanished in a swift blaze as urgency began to build in its place. Grady shoved Isaiah back and sat, ripping off his own shirt, vaguely conscious of Isaiah stripping near him. Grady's hands were on the button of his jeans when he looked up. His fingers forgot how to work as he stared at Isaiah with an open mouth.

There was quite possibly some drool involved, as well. Damn. Just...damn.

Grady had seen Isaiah's body before. You couldn't work on a ranch and not end up catching at least a few glimpses of chest, if not more. But he didn't remember Isaiah looking quite so edible. His body was lean, almost skinny next to Grady's far more considerable bulk. But what he lacked in size he more than made up for with the sculpted cut of his slender muscles. The fuzz on his chest and stomach was darker than his hair, and far more plentiful than Grady would have expected, particularly around his groin. Like the rest of Isaiah, his cock was long and thin, hard and just begging to be touched. Grady took his hands away from the fastening of Isaiah's jeans to tunnel them through the wiry curls.

"Damn, you're something." Grady had to swallow before his voice would work properly. Even then, it was hoarse and low.

"I'd like to be able to say the same thing about you, but you're still wearing too many clothes."

Oh. So he was. Unfortunately, Grady couldn't seem to make himself stop touching his lover long enough to remedy the situation. Isaiah laughed and took care of the problem for him.

Grady's jeans hit the floor with a thump. Isaiah landed against him a moment later with about the same sound. Grady hummed happily at the feeling of that coarse hair rubbing against his chest. Isaiah nipped and licked at Grady's collarbone, the stubble from his five o'clock shadow scraping up the nerve endings in his skin, leaving a lovely tingle everywhere that Isaiah visited.

Grady reached around and cupped Isaiah's tight ass, squeezing and kneading, even going so far as to run his fingers up and down the crease. Isaiah moaned and arched into the touch.

"More, babe. Damn, that feels good."

It did. Very, very good.

They dropped back onto the bed, Grady on the bottom. Didn't matter either way — he was an equal-opportunity switch. Top, bottom or — on one memorable occasion — middle, didn't matter in the slightest. Grady just wanted something. The kisses and touches were marvellous, but they weren't nearly enough anymore.

Grady pulled away from devouring Isaiah's mouth again. "Lube," he gasped. "In the drawer. I need you, now."

"Good," Isaiah panted back. "'Cause I need you, too."

Grady suppressed an extremely unmanly whimper when Isaiah pulled away. Hell, even their skin tried to hold them together, gathering sweat making their flesh stick slightly Isaiah braced himself on his knees and leaned over to rummage through the drawer.

"Oh, shit!"

Isaiah overbalanced and crashed to one side, squashing Grady's legs beneath him. Grady cracked up, laughing so hard his eyes blurred.

"Careful," he cautioned, sitting up. He grabbed Isaiah's hip to steady the man from tumbling further. His hand went wandering, though, and somehow ended up wrapped around the base of Isaiah's cock. "I'd hate for you to damage this before I get to use it," he teased, giving Isaiah a squeeze.

"Cut it out." Isaiah's grumble wasn't really meant, though. A minute later he sat up fully, brandishing a condom and a nearly unused tube of lube with pride. "Hah! Got it."

All laughter drained away when Isaiah moved again, pinning Grady to the mattress.

"You sure about this?" Isaiah asked seriously. "Because once I start, I'm not going to stop, and I'm damn sure not going to want to give you up. So if this is just a one-time thing for you, tell me now."

Grady's mouth went dry. He licked his lips, panic beginning to rise in him. But in the end, there was really only one answer he could give Isaiah.

When words wouldn't come, Grady just nodded his head against the pillow.

Isaiah muttered a low, "Thank God." He settled himself more securely between Grady's legs and dipped down for another kiss. Grady let his hands go wandering again, up over Isaiah's chiselled abs to seek out the hard nipples. He stroked with his thumbs and was rewarded by a deep groan and another kiss.

"Lift up, babe," Isaiah urged. Grady obeyed, shifting his weight and spreading his legs. Isaiah groaned again.

"Look at that," he murmured. He wrapped one hand around Grady's thigh to hold him steady while tracing an exploratory circle around his ass hole with the other. Grady couldn't prevent the involuntary squeeze when the tip of Isaiah's finger penetrated the tight ring of muscle.

"Sorry," he said. "It's been a while."

"I can tell," Isaiah replied distractedly. "I'll go slow."

"Not too slow."

Isaiah's smile was wicked and hinted at all kinds of spine-tingling delights. "No, not too slow," he promised.

Grady hissed at the cold swipe of gel as Isaiah lubed him up. Isaiah apologised absently, intent on what he was doing.

"I'll warm you up in a minute," he assured Grady.

Grady didn't reply—too busy drowning in the sensation of Isaiah's fingers probing his ass. Grady felt one thick finger work its way deep and even that made him feel damn full. When Isaiah added a second finger, the pressure built.

And damn, did it ever feel good.

"More," Grady urged.

"You're too tight," Isaiah countered. "Just be patient."

"Patience be damned." Time to play dirty. Grady bore down on Isaiah's fingers, by turns sucking him in deeper and wrapping him in tighter. Isaiah cursed. That cursing grew louder and more vicious when Grady grabbed Isaiah's cock without preamble, stroking from base to tip. He couldn't resist gathering a bit of pre-cum off the top, swiping with swirling motions around the head. Then he *really* couldn't resist taking a taste. Grady brought his fingers to his lips, licking the wetness off, humming happily at the salty flavour.

"Oh, fuck."

Grady looked up to find Isaiah staring at him with wide eyes. His pupils were blown with arousal, swallowing nearly all traces of brown.

A third finger slammed into Grady's ass forcefully and he yelped—hips arching—not sure whether he wanted to get away from the touch or get closer.

"Don't you dare apologise again," he ordered Isaiah. "Just stop playing around."

Grady could have cried in relief when he heard the distinct, familiar sound of a wrapper being ripped open. He felt the removal of Isaiah's fingers with a deep sense of loss but an instant later, the blunt head of Isaiah's cock bumped against his hole.

"Now, please." Grady tugged on Isaiah's hair, dotting his chin with kisses.

"Then lay back down," Isaiah ordered.

Grady didn't even remember jacking upward to reach his lover's face, but he obeyed the order with alacrity. He let his legs fall open, splaying himself wide like some damn virgin sacrifice.

With slow, steady motions, Isaiah began to push in. Forward, back, rocking deeper with each shove.

"Stop teasing," Grady demanded.

"Not teasing," came the ragged reply. "Don't want to hurt you."

"You won't."

With that assurance, Isaiah's control broke. He surged forward in one jerky movement. Grady yelped, the burn of pain enough to make his cock soften a bit. *Damn.*

But the blast of pain was quickly driven away by pleasure as Isaiah rocked deep inside Grady, brushing against his prostate with every motion. Grady's moans of pleasure soon rose to cries of delight. That long, thin cock reached deeper inside than anything Grady could remember.

"Isaiah."

Isaiah took that as his sign, pulling almost completely out before slamming back in with enough force to inch Grady up the mattress. Grady wrapped his legs around Isaiah's lower back, throwing his head back, closing his eyes and enjoying the ride. Isaiah dropped his weight, bracing himself on his elbows. Grady's cock rubbed along Isaiah's stomach with every stroke, the abrasion of Isaiah's chest hair rough. It sent him higher, little spots dancing in front of his eyes.

"Soon," Isaiah panted. Sweat dampened his blond hair, making it darker, his lips tight. Then Grady gave a loud shout, muscles tensing as his lover shoved deeply inside, so deeply that Grady thought it was entirely possible that he would feel the man there for the rest of his life.

Isaiah stilled, back arching, as he rode out his climax. Grady watched in awe, transfixed by the tight features, the painful bliss plain on Isaiah's face.

Isaiah slumped and Grady moaned.

"Almost there," he pleaded.

Isaiah grunted, hand moving between them. He stroked Grady's cock once, twice, and Grady lost control. With a shout of his own, his climax ripped through him. His vision greyed out with the force of his body's release.

When it was over, they both slumped in a sweaty, exhausted pile.

"I think I'm ready for that shower now," Isaiah mumbled into Grady's shoulder.

"In about two days," Grady mumbled back. "When I can move again."

A low chuckle shook the bed. Isaiah used one hand to flop himself off Grady.

"Yeah, that sounds about right."

Grady was sticky and sweaty and filthy but he didn't care. Even the small specks of dried blood still on his arms didn't bother him in the slightest. Instead, he let Isaiah tuck him close and fell quickly into the most relaxed sleep he could remember having in ages.

This was where he was supposed to be. Where he needed to be. Right here, tucked up against the man who had made his life worth living again.

Chapter Seventeen

Isaiah hummed softly and rolled over. He was warm and comfy and...*cuddling*?

Oh. Oh, yeah. Without opening his eyes, Isaiah snuggled closer to the hot, hard body pressed up against him. Grady. Dillon. And sex and...yeah. *I could stay here, like this, for the next week or so. Would be good.*

Would be better if someone stopped pounding on the door.

He reluctantly untangled his limbs from Grady's, getting a sleepy, grunting protest as their hips bumped. Isaiah grinned, looking over the prone figure. How had he never known how damn cute Grady was when asleep? Well, he knew now, and it was a sight he definitely wanted to see again. Over and over and over.

Isaiah slid out from under the rumpled, skewed covers, trying not to waken his sleeping lover. Grady made another protesting noise and turned, clutching a pillow to his chest. Isaiah's grin felt like it was trying to crack his face, it was so wide. He shook his head, padding across the floor towards the door.

Oh, shit. Clothes. Yeah.

Isaiah backtracked and dug up a pair of jeans — they were a bit big, and he thought they might be Grady's, but they would do. He didn't intend to be up for long.

Decently covered, Isaiah swung open the door. A pair of curious green eyes blinked up at him.

Isaiah froze, everything in him tightening, mind blanking out. Shit. Josh. What to tell Josh?

"Umm —"

Josh grinned cheekily and gave him a thumbs-up.

"Little imp," Isaiah replied.

Josh shrugged and tried to peer around Isaiah. Isaiah ushered the boy back out into the hall, following so he could close the door behind them.

"Did you need something in particular?" Isaiah asked.

Josh raised one eyebrow and gave Isaiah one of his special 'Are you kidding me?' looks. The kid should patent those. Isaiah had never seen one better.

Josh pretended to look at a watch, giving Isaiah another look. One hand went to his mouth.

Feed me. *Oh, shit.* He should know better than to nap during the evening.

Isaiah groaned. "Sorry, kiddo. Hotdogs and mac and cheese okay? Grady's asleep and I don't want to wake him."

Josh wrinkled his nose, but then nodded his acceptance of the offer.

Isaiah tramped down the stairs behind the tyke, resisting the urge to smack himself on the forehead. What kind of lousy parent figure was he? Because truthfully, he'd completely forgotten about Josh.

Completely. Grady had stolen his focus and attention, absorbed him like a frickin' amoeba.

Now that Isaiah thought about it, though, he was pretty hungry, too. Sex would do that. In the kitchen he grabbed a package of hotdogs out of the fridge and pulled a familiar blue box from the cabinet. Then he shrugged and pulled down another. What the heck, the stuff went down easy.

When Isaiah put the pan of water on the stove, he caught a glimpse of the time on the display. He winced.

"Sorry," he apologised again. "I didn't mean to get so distracted."

God, he was a horrible parent. What made him think he could do this again? Oh, yeah. All it took was one look at that pixie face staring back at him with false innocence and Isaiah remembered. Damn. Why couldn't he have worked things out with Grady sooner? Like, years sooner? Trying to juggle the intricacies of parenthood and start up a new relationship all at the same time was really too much to ask of any one guy. Case in point, dinner at eight-thirty at night. A decidedly unhealthy dinner.

Josh enjoyed it, though. He scarfed down the food like he hadn't eaten in days. Since Isaiah had caught the kid raiding the fridge twice this afternoon, he knew differently. He chuckled.

"Slow down before you choke," Isaiah advised. "I don't know CPR. You'd be in trouble."

Josh made a face and shoved another forkful of yellow pasta into his mouth. One hand came up, finger poking, and twirling. It took Isaiah a minute to figure out the question, posed in a weird mix of ASL and Josh's own signals.

"You going to sleep with Grady now?"

"I hope so," Isaiah replied. "We haven't really talked about it. Rules haven't changed, though. You need me, you knock and I'll answer. You're still my first priority. Grady's, too, I'd bet. He's as attached to you as I am."

Isaiah almost missed the flash of relief that skittered across Josh's eyes. For a kid, he was far too skilled at disguising his emotions. If Isaiah hadn't seen the expression, he wouldn't have even known Josh had been worried.

Isaiah put down his fork and leant forward on his elbows. "Listen, Josh, I wish I could change your past, I really do." The uncertainty Josh would have lived with, the erratic schedule—hell, just dealing with his airhead mother, was really not a good situation for a kid, particularly one like Josh. Isaiah had talked to a few people when Josh had first moved in permanently. He'd even scheduled a few appointments with a psychologist over in Barton, just to ease some of the pressure and get some reassurance that he was doing the right thing by his little brother. Everyone had said the same thing—Josh needed continuity, a schedule, a sense of security. They probably wouldn't approve of Isaiah starting up a relationship, but in Isaiah's mind, it was another step in the right direction. One more link to tie Josh into their little family unit.

"Josh." Josh was staring into his bowl, trying to hide from Isaiah. Isaiah sighed and reached over, grabbed one small hand. "We love you, both of us. Nothing changes, except hopefully we're a stronger family. But I'll need your help. Maybe together, we can get Grady to stop hanging back."

Josh's eyes reflected such longing and hope that it made Isaiah's chest tighten. Grady had looked at him like that, too. Between the two of them, they were going to turn Isaiah into a big pile of mush. His reputation was going to be squashed.

Somehow, he didn't really care. If these two needed him to be mushy and talk about his feelings, that was what he would do. Now that he had them both, he wasn't going to give them up. Not without one hell of a fight.

Soft sounds made him look over to see a sleepy-eyed Grady hovering in the doorway.

"Any food left?" Grady asked with a quiet, almost shy, smile.

"I don't think so," Isaiah admitted. "The human garbage disposal pretty much decimated what I made."

"'S'okay," Grady replied around a yawn. "Not sure I'm all that hungry, anyway."

"There might be a hotdog left," Isaiah offered.

Josh took his bowl over to the sink, dumping it in and bouncing on his toes a bit. He stopped and gave Grady a tight hug before exiting the room with all the speed a ten-year-old could muster.

"Half hour," Isaiah called out after Josh. "Then to bed."

Grady watched him go with surprise. "What was that about?" he asked.

"I think that was his way of saying he's okay with us. You know, being together."

The plate Grady was holding hit the counter with a loud clatter, Isaiah winced, but it didn't break. "You told him?"

Isaiah raised one eyebrow. "We weren't exactly quiet. Besides, he found me in your room. Josh is far too smart not to connect the dots."

Grady groaned. "God, that's embarrassing."

"Nah," Isaiah said, standing and pulling Grady close. He wrapped his arms around Grady's waist and nuzzled at the sensitive skin at the base of his neck. "I think it's kinda cool."

"Not now." Grady's words didn't hold any conviction, though, and he didn't step away.

"Josh is busy," Isaiah countered. "And you smell really good."

Grady must have jumped in the shower. He smelt like soap, clean and fresh, and his thick hair was damp and curling at the ends. Isaiah nuzzled again, adding a little nip that he soothed with his tongue. Grady shuddered, his whole body swaying with the caress. Damn, but Grady was sensitive. It was such a turn-on—Isaiah couldn't remember ever having such a responsive lover. Grady seemed starved for it, soaking up each touch, each bit of affection, like it was something new and vital.

"Half-hour," Isaiah promised. He made himself step away before he took things too far. He was already aching and wanted nothing more than to throw Grady down on the table and munch on him like a buffet. But they had a kid in the other room and for what Isaiah wanted, he needed privacy and time. Lots and lots of time. Like all night.

Isaiah brushed Grady's cheek with another quick kiss. "Get something to eat," he encouraged. "You'll need your strength for later."

Grady groaned, a flush working up his tanned cheeks.

Isaiah grinned, unrepentant. "I'm going to go let the kid trounce my ass at some video games. Then we can put him to bed and start making up for lost time."

"You're evil." Grady's voice rasped a bit when he spoke, his eyes glazed with lust. Isaiah just laughed.

"Yep, that's me," he teased. "Evil. But hey, I more than make up for it. Just wait."

Grady growled and lunged at him. Isaiah took off, laughing the whole way.

True to his prediction, Josh beat him badly at some racing game. Isaiah gave it his best shot but the stupid car wouldn't cooperate. He spent more time trying to get himself unstuck from the rail than actually racing. Josh's snickers didn't help.

"Bed," he announced after nearly forty minutes of excruciating torture. "It is definitely time for bed."

Josh started to pout, but Isaiah gave him a stern look. Giving in with a sigh, Josh shut down the game and disappeared upstairs.

It didn't take Isaiah long to lock things up, turn out the lights, and make sure Josh was settled for the night. He said goodnight and made sure the bedroom door was open a crack. A quick detour by his bedroom to stock up, then Isaiah made his way back to Grady's room. This door, he closed all the way.

Grady was waiting for him. Isaiah stripped and slid under the covers with a sigh.

"Hey," he said softly.

"Hey," Grady echoed.

Isaiah settled in closer, dragging his fingertips along smooth skin.

Grady stilled his motions with one hand. Isaiah had to bite back a whimper at the serious expression he received.

"I need to know where this is going," Grady insisted quietly, but intensely.

"Where do you think it's going?" Isaiah asked sharply.

"I don't know, that's why I'm asking!"

Isaiah rolled his eyes, flipping the bigger man over in one swift move. He landed on top of that broad chest, making sure Grady looked him right in the eye and could see the utter sincerity he was feeling.

"I would be perfectly happy to lock us both inside this room and never come out again," he said sternly. "That answer your question?"

"So it's about sex."

"Good Lord, Dillon! Do you always have to jump to the worst possible conclusion?"

Grady looked away. Isaiah sighed and shifted his weight, but made certain to keep in close contact with his insecure lover. He hadn't meant to get into this so soon, but it was obvious that Grady needed the reassurance.

"Love doesn't always leap out of the bushes and whack you over the head with a branch," he explained apologetically. "Sometimes it sneaks into the house in the middle of the night and crawls into bed with you, and when you wake up the next morning you realise it's always been there. You were just too much of a blind idiot to see it."

"You...you love me?" Grady whispered, eyes wide in shock.

A fist clutched Isaiah's gut and he had to take several breaths until his body relaxed again. "You don't...care about me?" he asked quietly. He'd never known it was possible to feel such devastation.

Grady's head shook rapidly. "I've loved you for years," he confessed in a low, small voice. "Ever since that first roundup. You were stunning, so confident and assured, even though you had no clue what you were doing. You kept screwing up, but you just ignored the glares and laughed and tried again."

"Why didn't you ever say anything? Make a move?"

Grady shrugged, eyes sliding away. "You deserved better. You still do."

Isaiah nearly choked on his fury, wanting to slam his fist into something. Or someone. Preferably several someones. If it was the only thing he accomplished in his life, Isaiah was going to make Grady see his own worth. See himself as others saw him. As Isaiah saw him.

But now wasn't the time to pursue it. Only time would help this particular problem. Just as earlier in the barn, words alone weren't going to cut it.

Isaiah smiled gently, tried to lighten the mood. "Is that why you hired me?" he teased. "'Cause you liked what you saw?"

A small smile tipped up the corners of Grady's firm lips. Isaiah wanted to pump his fist into the air and yell 'Success!' but he managed to stifle the impulse.

"That might have been part of it," Grady admitted with a sheepish shrug. "But I've never regretted it."

"I'd always wondered a bit, why you hired me," Isaiah commented. "I have a literature degree, for God's sake. I knew horses, but I was clueless about cattle and running a ranch."

"You minored in business," Grady pointed out. "And I needed a business manager more than I needed a foreman. I knew cattle, and the rest you could learn. I just couldn't...with Tracy gone I couldn't keep up. The finances and paperwork were...I guess I was too stupid to —"

"I never want to hear those words come out of your mouth again," Isaiah said harshly.

"But it's the truth."

"Is Josh stupid?"

"Of course not!"

"He has a handicap, a disability that means there are certain things he can't do. Just like you. It doesn't mean you're stupid or worthless or any of those other ridiculous labels you keep pinning on yourself. It means you have to work harder than others, find creative ways to cope. It *doesn't* mean there's anything wrong with you."

Grady squeezed his eyes closed. "I'm so scared," he admitted hoarsely. "What if I can't live up to your expectations? What if I screw this up?"

"Enough, babe," Isaiah ordered. He tipped Grady's chin up and captured those slightly chapped lips into a deep kiss. "Push it all away for a while. Just let me love you. Everything else will work out."

Grady looked like he wanted to argue some more, but Isaiah was, once again, done talking. He shut Grady up the best way he knew how, with another passionate kiss. One kiss led to another, then another—both men's hands roaming freely. Isaiah stroked Grady's side, tilting his head from one side to the other, slanting their lips together. His tongue kept busy exploring, inside and out.

"Love me," Isaiah said fiercely. "Now, babe, I need you."

Grady started to turn over, and Isaiah stopped him.

"No," he said. "I need you in me."

Grady's eyes widened. "You sure?"

"Positive."

Grady scrambled for the supplies, digging out the familiar tube of lube and a condom. Isaiah took the lube but tossed the condom to one side.

"We don't need it," Isaiah said in answer to Grady's unspoken question. "I trust you. You're it for me. You wanted to know where this was going. Well, it's you and me, exclusive, until you kick me out."

"You're sure about this?"

"Yes. I got tested not long ago. I'm clean. The papers are in the office, if you want to —"

Grady shook his head and it was his turn to say, "I trust you. If you want this, then yes. Absolutely, yes."

Isaiah's grin was huge and probably a little bit wild. They switched places, Isaiah propping himself up against the pillows. He reached one hand down, slipping two well-lubed fingers into his ass. The burn ripped up his spine, the pain almost too much. He rarely bottomed. But he didn't want to wait. He wanted Grady in him, now.

Grady knelt between Isaiah's legs, his hungry gaze following every motion. Isaiah found the intensity to be one hell of a turn-on, especially when Grady reached out with one callused finger to trace the rim of his asshole.

"Damn, that feels good," Isaiah gasped, shoving in another finger. "Keep touching me, babe, please."

Grady obeyed, his touch a bit hesitant but oh so perfect.

"Can't...need you now, babe." Isaiah's breath was coming in gasps, his spine tingling. He arched into Grady's touch, pulling his fingers free. "Now, Dillon, now."

"You sure?" Grady asked with concern. "You only used two —"

Isaiah cut him off expediently with a hand to Grady's thick cock. He stroked up to the base, squeezing gently.

And still Grady hesitated. Isaiah rolled his eyes, patience gone. He grabbed Grady's shoulders and flipped him onto his back, straddling the bigger cowboy's waist.

"Fine," he huffed with fake annoyance. "I guess I'll just have to go riding."

"Riding? What?"

Isaiah let his body drop, thigh muscles taking the strain as he balanced himself and lined all the pieces up. Grady's cock nudged against his ass, slid into the crack. Almost...there...*perfect*!

Isaiah sat down, impaling himself on Grady's cock. Grady shouted, back arching, as his lubed cock drove into Isaiah's tight heat. Isaiah tossed his head back, regretting for a brief minute not stretching out more. Because damn, Grady was on the large side, and it bloody well...*oh, there. Right there.*

The thick head of Grady's penis rubbed across Isaiah's prostate and all the pain vanished. Pleasure swamped him, blinding him for a second. When it cleared, he looked down to a glorious sight. Grady lay splayed beneath him, eyes wide and almost blank, skin reddened with passion, chest heaving with each breath. The man looked utterly lost in sensation. Good, that was just the way Isaiah wanted him. Pleasure-drugged and unthinking.

Starting out slowly, Isaiah began to ride his lover, gaining speed with each motion. Up and down, he kept the rhythm erratic, wanting to draw this out as long as he could. They thrust and grunted, panted and swore, for endless minutes. Until their muscles were shaking and Isaiah's thighs, as hardened as they were from years of horse-back riding, began to scream a protest.

Isaiah shifted forward, bracing his hands on Grady's shoulders. He dropped down while Grady thrust up. Neither could form words anymore, bodies straining for release.

And then it came. Grady shouted wordlessly, slamming up into Isaiah with such force that Isaiah thought he was going to jam his cock into Isaiah's throat. Thick, hot cum flooded Isaiah's ass.

Isaiah gasped in shock at the feeling. He'd never had sex without a condom and the feel of Grady filling him up, spunk dribbling out of his ass, was incredible. The heat seared him and a sense of intimacy he'd never experienced nearly overwhelmed him. Isaiah dropped his head back, balls drawing up, tight and painful. When he moved forward again, his cock rubbed against Grady's stomach.

It was too much for over-sensitised skin.

"Dillon!" Isaiah's yell probably made it clear to the bunkhouse that his release was ripping through him. He sprayed the warm skin beneath him with his mark, wave after wave of pleasure jarring up his spine. Spots danced in his vision as the longest orgasm he'd ever experienced consumed him.

Isaiah could barely suck air into his lungs. He collapsed onto Grady, smearing spunk between them. The change in position caused Grady to grunt. Isaiah echoed the sound when Grady's cock jerked out of his sore ass.

"Damn," Isaiah said, when he finally managed to get enough air to speak. "I'm dead."

"Me, too," Grady said, patting Isaiah on the ass.

"Sorry if I'm squishing you," Isaiah said, "But I don't think I can move."

"You're good," Grady assured him.

"So are you," Isaiah teased.

A loud pounding shook the walls. Isaiah yelped and fell sideways, losing his precarious perch atop Grady.

"What the hell was that?" Isaiah demanded.

"I don't—"

The pounding sounded again. Grady groaned and suddenly buried his face into Isaiah's shoulder. "Oh, God, kill me now," he moaned.

"Maybe we should consider moving him to a different room," Isaiah replied dryly while Josh banged on the wall a third time. "I guess that means we're done for tonight."

He should probably be embarrassed or, at the least, feel bad that Josh had heard them. And maybe he would. Tomorrow. When he came back to life.

For now, Isaiah put any — and all problems — on the back burner before draping himself over his big lover. At the moment, he was too tired to even care that he was leaking cum all over the sheets.

"There's always the shower," he mumbled sleepily. "Loud water's good for cover."

Chapter Eighteen

Micah threw down his cards and scowled. "I fold."

Tommy chuckled gleefully and all but rubbed his hands together. "I am the king!" He spread his own cards out, crowing with delight at the disgusted expressions surrounding him.

Isaiah watched the action from his position in the doorway, trying to stifle his amusement. He was having too much fun observing to be noticed just yet. Josh snickered at Tommy.

"Oh no, you don't." Tommy glared back at the pint-sized card shark on the other side of the table. "That is just plain wrong, buddy."

Josh simply smiled wickedly and laid out four aces. Groans sounded all around the table and Joseph was laughing so hard he almost choked.

"That about does it for me," he declared. "I think the kid's wiped me out."

"We're playing for pennies," Micah drawled.

"Yeah. And I'm down ten bucks. Kid, you're gonna be deadly when you hit twenty-one."

Josh chortled and waggled his eyebrows, prompting another wave of laughter.

"I'm gonna get another drink," Joseph announced. "Anyone want something?"

He got a chorus of requests and Josh held up his empty glass imperiously.

"We're corrupting the child," Joseph said. Isaiah stepped aside to let Joseph by, getting a small nod of acknowledgement. None of the others paid any attention, not even when Joseph returned a few minutes later with an armful of drinks. He passed out beer bottles. "Chocolate milk for you," he added, refilling Josh's glass. Josh smiled happily and took a deep drink.

"You've got a moustache," Tommy pointed out. "I want one."

"There's more milk in the fridge," Joseph said absently. He stacked the cards and started to shuffle. "Another round, or are we done getting our asses whupped by a ten-year-old?"

"Oh, heck, I'm always up for more humiliation," Tommy said.

"Maybe we should try Go Fish," Micah suggested as Joseph started to deal out the cards. "We might have more luck."

Josh wrinkled his nose, sliding his pile closer.

"I guess that's a no," Micah said with a laugh. He finally spotted Isaiah and waved. Josh imitated the gesture.

Isaiah walked into the room, smiling at the small group. All his hands and his little brother sat at the round table, cards in hands, small piles of coins next to each person. The stack of pennies next to Josh was about six times the size of the rest.

"Hey, boss," Tommy called cheerfully.

"Should I be worried that you're all up here drinking and playing poker? With my kid brother?"

"Aw, we're just educating the kid." Tommy spoke again. "Besides, we're not giving him alcohol. He's got chocolate milk, lucky bugger."

"I told you, there's more in the refrigerator," Joseph said, studying his cards as if they held the secrets to life, liberty, and the pursuit of happiness.

Isaiah shook his head and straightened, coming farther into the room. He grabbed an empty chair and swung it around beforeplopping his butt down. He rested his arms on the ladder back.

"We can deal you in," Micah offered.

Isaiah shook his head. "I'm good."

"Three," Tommy announced.

"Pass."

Josh slid over four cards, taking four new ones. Isaiah looked askance and Tommy snickered.

"All right, I'm in." Joseph tossed some pennies on the table.

"Call."

Josh tossed in his own bet, adding a few pennies to the stack.

The round ended and they all displayed their cards. Josh grinned with wicked glee as he presented his straight flush.

Isaiah cracked up. "Getting your butts kicked?"

"Always," Tommy announced cheerfully. "Kid's got the darndest luck. He beats us, without fail, every week. It's great."

Only Tommy would think consistently losing at poker was great. Joseph rolled his eyes and Josh giggled.

"Private party, or can anyone join in?"

Isaiah turned his head to see Grady hovering in the doorway, uncertainty etched in every line of his body. He sent the man a warm smile.

"Come on in," he invited. He couldn't help licking his lips at the slight blush on Grady's cheeks, nearly buried underneath the stubble of his end-of-the-day beard. The big man had worn pretty much the same expression last night, in bed. And the images that flashed through his head were causing a somewhat embarrassing reaction in the lower regions. Isaiah squirmed a bit and pretended not to notice the curious looks coming his way. Dang, his own face felt warm. No way was he blushing. No. Way.

"More the merrier," Tommy agreed.

"I'm not playing," Isaiah murmured when Grady took a seat next to him. "But I'm having a marvellous time watching my brother slaughter the grown-ups. At the rate he's going, he'll have enough winnings in pennies to buy a car by the time he gets his licence."

"That's a lot of pennies," Grady remarked. After watching the next hand with Isaiah, though, he laughed. "Huh. You're not wrong."

"I think he's cheating," Tommy said.

"Tommy!" The voices blended until Isaiah wasn't quite sure who had spoken.

"What?" Tommy said, wrinkling his brow. "It's a time-honoured tradition. I, for one, am impressed. It takes more skill to be good at cheating at cards than it does to actually *be* good at cards."

Grady shook his head. "I will never in a million years understand how your mind works."

"That's okay," Tommy replied. "I don't understand it, either."

"Are you sure it even does work?" Joseph asked sarcastically.

"I resent that!" The declaration didn't have any heat in it, though. Isaiah had learnt pretty quickly that it took a whole heck of a lot to piss off Tommy. In fact, he couldn't recall ever seeing Tommy angry, or even offended. Words that would normally get a reaction from anyone else just seemed to roll off the large cowboy like water off an umbrella.

Josh raised his once again empty glass in the air and shook it. Isaiah smiled.

"I'll get you more, squirt," he said, standing. Josh nodded his thanks solemnly, busy counting his pennies.

"I'll come with you," Grady said hastily. "I could use a soda or something."

Isaiah tramped down the stairs, aware the entire time of the big man at his back. He could actually feel the heat sparking between them. Isaiah had never been so conscious of Grady before, or of the sexual tension that thrummed between them. It was like once he had given the lust acknowledgement, it had roared to life with full force.

Down in the kitchen, Grady opened up the refrigerator. Isaiah nearly laughed to see it was filled to the brim, mostly with beer, soda, and restaurant leftover containers. His guys were typical bachelors when it came to the kitchen.

"You want anything?" Grady called over his shoulder, head inside the appliance.

Isaiah pressed up against Grady and wrapped his arms around Grady's waist, leaning over to speak lowly in his ear. "You."

Grady groaned. "We can't do that here," he protested. But he pushed back against Isaiah.

"The guys are all busy upstairs," Isaiah wheedled. "Come on, just a kiss. I've missed you."

Grady looked back at Isaiah. "Isaiah, I saw you less than three hours ago."

"Yeah, but I haven't had a kiss since this morning. Please?" Isaiah did his best imitation of a begging puppy and was rewarded when Grady's eyes softened.

"All right," Grady replied in a husky voice. "But just one kiss."

Of course, one kiss turned into two, then three. Before Isaiah was conscious of it, he had Grady pinned against the counter, hands up inside the man's shirt, devouring Grady's mouth like a starving man at a buffet. The kiss was explosive and heart-stopping and damn, Isaiah was going to come in his jeans. From a kiss. Who knew?

A throat cleared behind them. Grady stiffened in Isaiah's embrace, fingers digging into Isaiah's shoulders painfully. Isaiah reluctantly tore his lips from Grady's and turned his head.

Tommy stood a few feet away, expression unashamed, completely innocent, and with an irritating air of delight.

"Sorry to interrupt," he declared. "But his majesty is getting impatient for more chocolate milk. I want some, too, so I thought to come down here and see what was taking so long. So, I saw. And if you'll just hand me the milk, I let you get back to…that…" He ended with a wave of his hand.

"Um…Tommy…look, it's…" Isaiah had no clue what his stammering words were trying to be, but Tommy just rolled his eyes.

"Oh, come on, boss. Bosses. Everybody knows you've had a thing for each other. We've had a betting pool going on how long you would last before giving in. Gotta say, you went a heck of a lot longer than we thought. Winner's gonna make out good, but darned if I even remember who that is, it's been so long."

"Umm, sorry?" Isaiah really had no idea what to say. Still locked in his arms, Grady was silent and motionless and it worried Isaiah. Who knew what sort of hair-brained idea the man had now? It had taken Isaiah long enough to talk the man into something in the first place. Logically, they had both known they couldn't hide their relationship. Heck, Isaiah didn't even want to try. But Grady was hardly ready for this.

"Tommy!"

"Coming!" Tommy bellowed back at the voice from upstairs. "Milk?"

Isaiah leaned over, making sure to keep a grip on Grady's arm, and passed the milk over. He'd got it as far as the counter. Tommy took the carton and saluted them with it.

"Carry on," he said with stern sobriety. Then he cracked up and his laughter chased him all the way upstairs.

Isaiah groaned. "Is it just me, or does that guy get nuttier every day?"

"It's not you," Grady replied, but his voice was hoarse and he choked a bit on the words. "Isaiah?"

Isaiah sighed and rested his forehead on Grady's, looking down into worried hazel eyes. "Stop fretting, Dillon," he ordered. "You know our guys as well as I do. They won't have a problem with this. So get rid of whatever crazy thoughts are forming in your head. I don't want to have to go through this again. You're mine, I'm yours, no argument."

"I... Well, I know the guys won't give us trouble," Grady said by way of an apology. "But eventually word's gonna get out. Then what?"

Isaiah bit back a groan. "Do we have to talk about this right now? I was enjoying myself. I'd kind of like to finish what we started."

"We were only going to kiss. Once. Which we did, so technically we are finished. And we have to talk about it sometime."

"Later, babe, please?" Isaiah leaned over and pressed his lips briefly to Grady's. The scrape of stubble and the salty taste sent another pang of lust down to his cock, which was still throbbing from the earlier incendiary kiss. Tommy's appearance had dampened his arousal, but it hadn't killed it off entirely.

"Isaiah, we should—" Grady broke off, pressing back into the kiss. "All right," he finally said. "But we will have to talk about it eventually."

"Later," Isaiah promised. His tongue traced the seal of Grady's mouth until the man opened with a low moan, surrendering completely. Isaiah hummed his pleasure, pressing closer, their cocks rubbing and bumping through the thick fabric of their jeans.

"I can't wait to get you back in bed," Isaiah murmured, breaking the kiss to trail kisses along the scratchy jaw, continuing farther down to map the defined muscles of Grady's stomach before sliding around to trace small patterns on his lower back. "You're like nothing else I've ever experienced, like no one else I've ever touched."

"Damn right," Grady growled, and was that a hint of possession in his tone? It was, and Isaiah decided that he kind of liked it. He just had to give the man another toe-curling kiss in reward.

"Nobody like me," Grady gasped when they came up for air. "And you better remember it. I don't share."

"That goes both ways." Isaiah felt a little growly, himself, at the thought of Grady in someone else's arms. What they had, it was serious, at least for him. Serious and permanent. He had no intention of giving up the man in his arms, not anytime soon — possibly not ever.

"Hmm. Absolutely."

The kiss calmed, became lazier and gentler. Isaiah nipped and licked at the pliant lips beneath his, their tongues rubbing and swirling. He still wanted to come, badly, but it was more distant now. Tommy's presence had done one thing, it had reminded him that they weren't actually alone. Besides, he wanted to wait. Isaiah moved one hand down to grab Grady's tight little ass. He pressed their lower bodies together but resisted the urge to hump and buck. Instead, he used the ever gentling kisses to try to bring himself back under control. It probably wasn't the best idea he'd ever had, but Isaiah wasn't quite ready to let go of Grady. The man just tasted so damn good.

Grady was the first to pull away. He rested his head on Isaiah's shoulder, his breathing ragged and muscles trembling a bit with the effort of holding back. "We should probably go back upstairs," he whispered.

"Yeah."

Neither one of them moved. They stood there, Grady half-sitting on the counter, their arms wrapped around each other. Isaiah was content, completely so, and the little unconscious half-smile on Grady's face said he felt the same. Isaiah wouldn't have minded staying there, right like that, for the next hour or so. Of course, his body wouldn't let him. His cock would eventually gain the upper hand and he'd have to do something about it.

He knew the guys wouldn't let him, either. It was growing late and the cowboys were all like little mothers. They knew Josh's bedtime and were almost fanatical about it, particularly on weeknights. That was the one thing about taking Josh in that Isaiah hadn't expected. He'd thought he'd be on his own. Instead of gaining one parent figure, though, Josh had gained five. The boys had taken to their roles of honorary uncles with utter enthusiasm.

A thud sounded upstairs, followed by a loud collective groan. Grady chuckled.

"Sounds like Josh won again."

Isaiah grinned, squeezing his lover tightly before releasing him and stepping back. "Yeah. We'd best go congratulate the little pipsqueak. Grab your soda, babe. Time to go be social."

"Humph. I don't want to be social."

Isaiah just had to drop a kiss on the top of the man's head. Grady would deny it vehemently, but the man did have the cutest pout. "Social now, sex later," he promised.

"I'll hold you to that."

Grady grabbed a can of Coke and they headed back upstairs to join the others and watch Josh rule supreme at poker. Little by little, Isaiah was determined to drag Grady into the makeshift family he had created. No matter how much the man kicked and screamed. But judging by the smile on the man's face, the happy light in his eyes, Isaiah rather thought there wouldn't be all that much kicking and screaming.

Chapter Nineteen

"Hey, big guy." Isaiah closed the office door behind him and even took a second to make sure it was locked. Then he crossed the room and dropped a quick kiss on his lover's lips. As always, a quick kiss turned into something more. Then they were both laid out on the couch, touching and humping and having a grand old time.

Isaiah pulled back to take a breath. "Damn, babe. You get any better at this, I'm gonna have a heart attack."

"No heart attacks." Grady leaned in and kissed Isaiah on the neck. He ended the gentle caress with a sharp nip that had Isaiah arching into Grady.

"Damn," he gasped again. "Liked that. Do it some more."

Grady obliged, nibbling on Isaiah's skin like he was a big ol' juicy rib.

"What brings you to the house in the middle of the day?" Grady asked between bites.

"Huh?" The man expected him to *think?* Isaiah shook his head, but thought remained elusive.

Grady pressed down more firmly, squishing Isaiah into the couch cushions. It was a delicious pressure, especially when one thick thigh settled between Isaiah's legs.

"Shit."

Isaiah tugged his hands free. At some point, Grady had stretched his arms up and was holding him down. The position gave him the chills. Might be something to explore.

Later.

For now, Isaiah settled for opening Grady's jeans, then his own. He pushed fabric aside until he could get to hot, slick skin. With a low groan, Isaiah rubbed their cocks together. They didn't have a lot of time, but that was okay, 'cause the friction was right and perfect and...

"Shit." Isaiah's brain seemed to be stuck on that one word as he arched and writhed against Grady. Grady couldn't seem to find words at all, just a delightful series of moans.

Grady shifted his weight until he lay nearly flush along Isaiah, their lower bodies humping together with shallow, tight motions. Grady's lips, when they met Isaiah's again, were hot and swollen. Isaiah bit gently on Grady's lower lip, sucked on his tongue, and kept moving.

His climax hit with no warning. He stiffened, arching up, muscles going all tight as the pleasure ripped from his balls to his head.

"Shit."

Grady groaned, still moving, as Isaiah soaked his groin with his seed. One more long, deep kiss, and molten liquid splashed against Isaiah as Grady found his own release.

They lay pressed together and panted heavily.

"Gonna have to move soon," Grady murmured. "Or else we'll get stuck here."

The big guy had a point.

Isaiah shoved at Grady's chest until Grady took the hint and wiggled slowly to one side. Isaiah made a face, grimacing at the feel of sticky gunk coating his skin.

"Love the during," he muttered. "Hate the aftermath."

"What?"

"Nothing."

If he stretched just so, Isaiah could snag the tissue box with the tips of his fingers. It only took a minute to wipe off the evidence of their afternoon hook-up.

"I think we need to make this a habit," Isaiah said when they were all clean and dry. "Makes me nice and relaxed."

"Hmm. Good for you. Makes me sleepy."

Isaiah looked up into Grady's half-closed eyes and laughed. "Too bad, cowboy, we've got work to do."

He slapped Grady's hip. The man grumbled, but moved reluctantly off the couch, freeing Isaiah to do the same.

Isaiah couldn't remember ever being this happy. Grady seemed happy, too, more light-hearted than before, definitely smiling more. Heck, the big guy even laughed more now, and not just when Josh was around. Each time warmed Isaiah up inside.

Isaiah stood and took another kiss. "I should get back to work," he said quietly.

"I guess."

Isaiah was halfway across the room when Grady called after him.

"What did you come in here for, anyway?"

Isaiah smacked himself in the forehead. "God, I'm an idiot." He turned back around. "I needed the bill of sale on Mariah. Was talking to Mark Justice earlier today and he's got a stud would make a good match. I need a peek at her line, make sure we don't have any conflicts."

"I don't think so." Grady wandered to the filing cabinet and started rustling papers. The registrations and bills of sale were all kept together in the top drawer, colour-coded and everything. He tossed a folder on the desk. "Should be in there."

"Thanks."

Isaiah scooped up the whole pile and once again turned to leave.

"Oh, the mail's on the desk." Grady snagged the small pile, plucking a white envelope off the stack and waving it in the air. "This one looks kinda important."

Isaiah rolled his eyes. "Yeah, 'cause the last thing I need is more legal crap. Swear to God, it's a conspiracy. Forms are out to take over the world."

"I don't think it's the forms to blame," Grady said with a chuckle.

Isaiah grinned back. Damn, he liked that sound. He ripped open the envelope, not really paying attention, too focused on Grady's smile.

He should have known the bubble wouldn't last. Isaiah looked down at the official-looking stationary and cursed loudly. He was *happy*, damn it. Why the hell did people feel it was their right to interfere?

"This is ridiculous!" Isaiah shouted, anger welling up inside until he understood where the phrase 'seeing red' had come from. He tossed the offending piece of paper on the table and raked his hands through his hair, tugging hard. The bite of pain didn't distract him from the anger tearing through him.

Grady scooped up the paper and glanced at it, but looked to Isaiah for explanation.

"They're threatening legal action."

"Who?"

"The whole damn town! The Mayor and the Sheriff and the County Commissioner, and God only knows who else. They want to take Josh."

"What the hell?" Grady's eyes went dark and stormy. "They can't do that, can they?"

"Damned if I know."

"Why can't they just leave us alone?" Grady asked. His voice was small, quiet. He looked so vulnerable at that moment that Isaiah felt his anger increase twofold towards the bastards who'd brought this side of his lover out again. "We're not hurting anyone."

"No, we're not. You never have. They're bastards who don't give a damn who they hurt, as long as they're hurting *someone*."

"It's not fair to you," Grady continued, not even seeming to hear Isaiah's words. "You or Josh. Maybe we should just—"

"Oh, hell no," Isaiah bellowed. "I'm not giving you up."

"But they won't give up, either," Grady insisted, lips pressing together in a harsh line. "You know that." He gestured at the letter.

Spelled out in stark black was a warning, straight from the mayor's office in Edmonton. They were concerned about the so-called 'negative environment' fostered at the Branch. If changes weren't made, the letter said, the mayor would be forced to take action.

There was an innocent child involved. Social Services would be contacted, possible charges levied...

What the hell kind of charges you could make against a man raising his brother, Isaiah didn't know, but he didn't doubt that the good people of Edmonton would come up with something.

It was the involvement of Social Services that concerned Isaiah. He didn't know what the procedure was, what the rules were. He wasn't a complete idiot and he'd heard the stories. Heard about the prejudices in the system against gays. As much as it rankled, Isaiah wasn't about to let anything happen to Josh.

Isaiah sighed, not quite able to bring himself to look at Grady again, to see the pain in those darkened hazel eyes. He just didn't know what to do. He didn't want to give up Grady. But he didn't want Josh caught in the crossfire, either. It was a hell of a situation. Grady had the right of it. Why couldn't people just leave them in peace? They weren't hurting anybody. Josh was happy and healthy. What right did outsiders have to get involved in their world? Sure, they had an unconventional home and an unconventional family. Who didn't these days? It didn't make their way of life wrong or detrimental. Just different. Josh was getting love and affection, and being cared for the best they possibly could. That was the important thing. Wasn't it?

"Isaiah?"

Isaiah sighed, hand going to the back of his neck in that nervous gesture he could never quite get rid of. "I don't know what to do," he said quietly. "I just don't know."

Grady heaved a long sigh. "I wish I had an easy answer, but I don't think there is one." He paused, then asked, "Do you think they're right? That maybe this isn't the best thing for Josh? That *we* aren't the best thing for Josh? Together, I mean?"

Isaiah's jaw clenched so hard he heard his teeth snap together. "I don't see why not," he replied stubbornly.

"We're two gay guys, Isaiah," Grady persisted. "Doesn't he deserve an actual family, mom and dad and siblings? The whole bit?"

"Just where the hell is he going to get that?" Isaiah snapped. "Besides, nothing says he'll never have siblings. I don't see how us breaking up, giving in to those damn bigots, is going to make the slightest bit of difference."

"No, probably not," Grady conceded the point with a distinct lack of conviction. He skirted the table holding the letter like it was a box of venomous snakes. His big body pressed close to Isaiah's, wrapping his arms around Isaiah's shoulders. He dropped his head forward until their foreheads touched and he stared solemnly into Isaiah's eyes. Isaiah's gut churned. He knew what was coming.

"I love you," Grady whispered, voice cracking and full of pain. "And Josh. You both mean the world to me. And I can't risk the hurt that this would cause. I can't risk something happening to him. I love you too much to stand beside you and watch this town rip you both apart."

"You mean the way they've ripped you apart for years?"

"Exactly. I know better than anyone what kind of cruelty this town can be capable of. These aren't empty threats."

"Why do they hate you so much?" Isaiah asked gently.

Grady's eyes slid away. "I don't know," he confessed. "I've never known. Doesn't really matter, either."

"No, I guess not." Isaiah wrapped his arms around Grady, hugging the now familiar bulk of his lover close.

Something inside him was shattering, a piece of his soul ripping away. The threats weren't empty ones. The mayor and the town council and God only knew how many other people would drag Social Services into it. Maybe Grady and Isaiah could fight back, keep custody of Josh. But was the cost too high? The uncertainty and the stress and the trauma—it would hurt Josh in ways Isaiah could only imagine.

Isaiah was selfish, too. Maybe they could win. But then again, maybe they couldn't. Isaiah wasn't certain he could take that chance.

Isaiah's arms tightened around Grady. Grady returned the embrace, a shudder ripping through him.

"I'm gonna miss you guys so much," he whispered into Isaiah's neck.

"I haven't said I'm going anywhere." But Isaiah's voice broke midsentence. He needed to stop and *think*. Just for a minute. But the emotions weren't letting him. Isaiah's eyes stung as he inhaled the smell of leather and Grady's cologne and, under that, the scent that was Grady's alone. The thought that he wouldn't be able to hold this man, spend all day playing in bed together, or ride fence line, laughing and joking. Never go to the movies, just the three of them. Scenes flashed through his head, of all the things they'd done together and would never do again. Of all the things they had planned to do and now never would. Goddamn it, would they even get Christmas together?

"Where will you go?"

"Maybe we'll head back to California for a bit," Isaiah said after a long pause. "Just for a bit, until things die down and I figure out where I stand, legally."

Isaiah squeezed his eyes closed to hold back tears. He probably would have stayed there, just like that, except Grady muttered a low, vicious curse.

Isaiah's head came up and he nearly echoed that curse. Josh stood in the doorway of the study, green eyes huge and brimming with pain.

"Josh, how long have you —"

The venomous look Isaiah received cut off his words. Okay, a while then. Too long.

"Josh, it's not —"

Grady was having his own trouble finishing sentences, this time because big, silent tears started rolling down Josh's cheeks, which were reddened from the cold. Heck, the kid even still had his gloves on.

Josh suddenly darted across the room and flung himself at them, wrapping his little arms around Grady's legs and practically trying to climb the man like a tree. Grady let go of Isaiah to scoop up Josh. Isaiah pulled them both close, tucking Josh and Grady into a three-way hug with Josh sandwiched firmly in the middle.

"It's gonna be okay, kiddo," Grady whispered. "You'll see. You've got Isaiah to look after you. Sometimes real life doesn't get that storybook happy ending, and I'm sorry for that, more than you'll ever know. Just remember that I love you. I'll always love you. Both of you."

Josh's choked sobs were ripping Isaiah apart — they were even worse to bear than the thought of leaving Grady and the Branch. He and Grady shared helpless looks. Clearly, neither of them had the slightest idea how to fix this for Josh. It was going to be brutal, on all of them.

"I'm so sorry, Josh," Isaiah whispered.

Josh pulled back, wiping his eyes on the sleeve of his coat. He glared, shaking his head so violently the hood of his coat smacked Grady in the face. Josh reached out for Grady and clung tightly to the man's large, callused hands.

"I know you don't want to leave," Isaiah said. "I don't either. But it won't be forever, promise. There are..." Isaiah paused and sighed. How could he explain something like this to a ten-year-old? Isaiah took a deep breath and tried, anyway. "Some people don't like people like me and Grady."

Josh wrinkled his forehead in confusion. His little nose scrunched up with the expression.

"Grady and I... Well, it's not common..." Isaiah bit back a curse.

"Look at me, Josh." Grady once again came to his rescue. Dang it, how the heck was Isaiah going to get along without Grady to help him out? Despite the lack of kids in his life, Grady showed far more developed parenting skills than Isaiah on a frequent basis.

"What Isaiah is trying to say is that people don't like things that are different. And they really don't like people who are different. I think you know what I mean about that. In this case, it's normal for a boy and girl to like each other. Not two boys. People don't approve of our little family. They think a little boy should have a mom and a dad, not two dads."

Josh pulled back, hands moving, echoing both Grady and Isaiah's earlier thoughts. *Why should they care?*

"They just do," Isaiah said. "They're causing trouble over it. And as much as I hate it and think it's very, very wrong, there are things they can do about it. It's possible they could even get you taken away from me."

That thought clearly lit a small flame of panic in Josh, shown in his face and the almost frantic movements of his hands.

"I won't let that happen," he assured Josh. "But it means we'll probably have to leave and find somewhere else to live. For a while, anyway."

That panic grew, his hands moving until Isaiah couldn't follow the flow of thoughts anymore. Josh squirmed, forcing the two men to either put him down or drop him. Once back on the ground, Josh stomped one thick snow boot on the carpet. His face contorted into a mulish scowl.

"I know you don't want to leave," Isaiah said. "I don't either. But—"

Josh shook his head again, lower lip shoving out. He stomped his foot again.

A sudden surge of frustration caught Isaiah by surprise. Damn it all, did Josh think he *wanted* to do this? Isaiah was hurting just as much as Josh was. He'd just got Grady, and now he had to give him up. All because some utter bastards couldn't leave well enough alone, couldn't accept a gay couple in their midst, particularly one raising a child.

"Josh—"

Isaiah found himself the recipient of another venomous glare, one that lasted mere seconds before Josh whirled around and ran from the room. Isaiah met Grady's eyes as they heard pounding on the stairs, then the slamming of a door.

"I guess I should go talk to him," Isaiah said.

"I'm not sure what else there is to say, Isaiah," Grady replied. "You're both leaving, none of us likes it, what good will more talking do? Give him some time. He probably just wants to be alone for a while right now. I know I do."

"Grady—"

Grady shook his head, taking a step back when Isaiah reached for him again. "No. I know this is the right thing to do. I know you both have to leave. But I don't have to like it and I'm more than entitled to wallow in my misery for a while. You don't need to see that."

Grady vanished into the hallway after Josh. Isaiah dragged his hand down his face. Damn it. He wished for an instant that he was Josh's age. Then he could just throw himself onto the floor and have himself a major temper tantrum, complete with kicking feet and screamed denials until his voice gave out.

He was an adult. He had to act like one. No matter how much he didn't want to.

Isaiah was a doer, though. Oh, he tried. Somehow, he managed to keep himself confined to the study for a whole thirty minutes. Then his resolve broke and he tramped upstairs to find Josh, to at least give him a big hug. Maybe they'd feel better if they could just have a big cry together.

He was halfway up the stairs when he froze, earlier panic giving way to utter fury. What the hell was he doing? His only excuse—no, there was no excuse. They weren't wrong, the good people of Edmonton were, and it wasn't like Isaiah to give up without fighting back. Damn, Grady's pessimism must have rubbed off a bit. After all that work, getting Josh set up in a good school and pinning Grady down into a relationship, rebuilding his life around a new family unit, was he really just going to turn tail and run at the first rumblings of trouble?

Hell, no. Okay, grab Josh first. Then find Grady. Comfort his guys, make a plan. He could do this. They could figure out something, find some leverage. Grady'd lived here his whole life. Surely he had some dirt on the right honourable mayor. And the Sheriff, Isaiah knew first-hand that the Sheriff was a good man. A bit stiff-necked, a bit old-fashioned, but a good man nonetheless.

Information. He needed information. If Social Services did get involved, what were his rights? Heck, for all he knew, he could be panicking over nothing. Could be that the government couldn't care less about Josh living there, with them. A new sense of determination washed over him and he straightened, finishing the trek to the second floor.

"Hey, Josh?" Isaiah called from the doorway of Josh's room. It looked so different from even a few weeks ago. A thick comforter with a printed scene of running horses had replaced the old blanket Grady had used before. Posters were plastered all over the walls, horses and cowboy portraits. The Duke stared out over the desk from an old movie poster. Isaiah didn't even know where Josh had got most of them, but they painted a clear image of the boy his brother had become.

The low glow from the table lamp illuminated a huddled pile of covers on the bed. Isaiah flicked on the overhead light. "Josh, you wanna talk?"

Stupid question. Of course Josh didn't want to talk, even if he could. Isaiah had never seen his brother so angry. Worse than the anger, though, had been the hurt.

Isaiah sighed and rubbed the back of his neck. "Look, we handled that all wrong downstairs. Grady and me, I mean. We both panicked and jumped to worst-case obsession and —"

It suddenly occurred to Isaiah that he might as well be talking to a wall. He moved across the room, strides jerky. He leaned over to yank back the covers. "Josh, will you just…"

He stared in consternation, having trouble processing what he was seeing. Empty sheets, not even the imprint of a little body.

"Grady!" he bellowed.

Chapter Twenty

Grady had never heard quite that tone of sheer hysteria in Isaiah's voice. He dropped his glass in the sink, not even caring when it shattered. He pounded up the stairs and rounded the corner to find Isaiah standing beside Josh's bed, one edge of the covers in his hand.

"He's not here," Isaiah burst out, breath rapid and a touch ragged. "He went upstairs, I know he did, but he's not here!"

"Calm down, Isaiah." Grady did his best to try to soothe Isaiah, despite the fact that his own heart rate increased in sheer fright. "No need to panic just yet. Let's check the stables and the bunkhouse before we get all worked up. Heck, let's start by checking the rest of the house first."

Isaiah took a couple of deep breaths, visibly trying to regain some semblance of equilibrium. "Right. Check the usual places. I'm sure he just went to hide out with the horses. It's what he does, right?"

"Right. You head out there. I'll check the rest of the house and give the boys a call."

Isaiah was down the stairs and out of the door before Grady could finish his sentence. Grady stopped by their — his — room for his cell phone, dialling as he walked quickly through the house.

"Yo."

"Tommy, is Josh over there?"

"No, why?"

"Isaiah's checking the barn, but he's AWOL. We told him...well, he was really upset."

"On the way. Joseph!"

Tommy hung up, leaving the sound of his roaring shouts ringing in Grady's ears. Just the knowledge that the boys were on their way to help look eased some of the tightness in his chest.

That tightness came back with a vengeance, though, when he finally tracked Isaiah down in the main barn. Grady wordlessly handed over Isaiah's coat, which he had left behind in his mad dash. The barn creaked and groaned as the wind battered the siding. It looked like a snowstorm was moving in. Grady finished zipping his coat and pulled his gloves out of his pockets.

"No luck?"

Isaiah shook his head, jaw clenched and eyes frantic.

"All right, the boys are on their way. I'm gonna make a couple of calls."

"Who the hell are you gonna call?"

Grady bit his lip. "Isaiah—"

"No! Hell no! They're to blame in the first place!"

"Isaiah, if he is out there in this, we're going to need everyone we can get."

Isaiah shoved his arms into his coat and stalked to the door of the barn. "Do what you want. I'm not just sitting here."

"You need to wait. We don't have the first clue where to look," Grady argued. "You won't do Josh any good running around blind."

"And I'm not going to just stay here while he's out there, cold and lonely and probably lost!"

Tommy walked out of the gloom and wrapped one big arm around Isaiah's shoulders, pulling him close. "It's okay, boss. We'll find him, I swear."

Micah entered behind Tommy, stomping snow off his boots. "I've got a couple of horses saddled. We'll scout around, see if we can't find some kind of trail before the snow starts dumping. Joseph is checking over the snowmobiles."

"Thanks, Micah."

Grady understood Isaiah's distress, he really did. Grady felt the same. The thought of Josh outside in the path of an incoming storm, alone and hurt, made bile rise in his throat. But the only way to make sure their kid got home safe and sound was to keep a cool head. Isaiah's judgement was shot all to hell right now, so it was up to Grady to be the logical one.

Grady had to pull off one of his gloves to dial the number. "Lydia, it's Dillon Grady. Put Sheriff Thompson on the phone, please."

"He's not taking your calls." Lydia Mathesin, Everson County Dispatcher, sounded apologetic when she imparted that particular bit of not unsurprising news.

"Lydia, I don't care what sort of issues that jerk has — I've got an emergency out here."

"Grady, I can't —"

"Josh Preston is missing."

"Oh. Just one minute."

A click sounded and Grady waited impatiently, but he already felt a bit better. If he knew anything about

Lydia, she was already calling up the rest of the volunteer search and rescue team. And probably everybody on her Christmas card list for good measure. The woman was close to a saint with a heart of gold. It reminded Grady that not everyone in Edmonton hated him. Some people were actually decent and didn't give a shit who you slept with.

"Thompson."

"Sheriff, this is Dillon Grady."

"I told Lydia—"

"Don't be an ass," Grady interrupted harshly. "I've got a missing kid and no time for bullshit."

The Sheriff might be a prick and one of the people who instigated the whole mess, but he wasn't heartless and he was good at his job. He agreed to call in his deputies and head their way, but made no promises.

"The weather's already getting nasty here and it's coming your direction. I don't have enough equipment to get my whole department in."

"We'll take whatever we can get," Grady assured him. "Thanks."

"That's my job," Thompson said gruffly. "Besides, he's just a kid."

Grady hung up with a relieved sigh. Tommy and Micah were watching him with anxious expressions. Isaiah was nowhere to be seen.

"Backup's on the way. Where'd Isaiah go?"

"To help Joseph with the snowmobiles."

"All right." They only had two. Horses worked just as well most of the time. "You two head out and take a look. I'll try to keep Isaiah from doing something stupid."

* * * *

By the time Thompson pulled up—lights on his SUV casting eerie blue and red shadows over the snow-covered ground—Grady sported a sore jaw and a black eye and Isaiah's knuckles were bruised. But Grady had won the argument and Isaiah was still on the ranch, so Grady wasn't complaining.

The Sheriff nodded to them and listened carefully while they explained what had happened. Micah and Tommy had found tracks—boot prints, unfortunately—heading west. Grady wished like hell Josh had at least taken one of the horses. It would have provided some extra warmth to the skinny little boy. They'd followed Josh's prints about a mile before the increasing wind had wiped the land clean. With the snow now falling in fat flakes, any chance of following a trail had vanished. The darkening clouds moving in slow procession overhead created a false twilight that soon dropped a gloom around the buildings that no lights could pierce.

The yard quickly became crowded with vehicles of all kinds. A couple of the local ranchers even showed up on horseback. Grady was actually a bit surprised by how many people had arrived. But then again, maybe he shouldn't be. They might hate his guts and, by extension, Isaiah's, but all bets were off when a kid was involved. And with Josh, well, he had a knack for making friends. Few people could resist his bright smile and easy charm.

Thompson spread a map out on the hood of his SUV and plotted out grids by the scattered glow of dozens of headlights.

"We can't risk missing any sections," he said. "And I want everyone in pairs. This weather is only going to get worse. So don't take any unnecessary risks and pack it in if it gets dangerous. I want to find that boy, but not at the cost of lives, got it?"

A round of agreement met him, but Grady could tell, by the looks on some people's faces, that it was a token agreement at best. His men and Isaiah, for sure, weren't going to stop until they found Josh, risk be damned. Hell, Grady wasn't either.

Thompson passed out radios, then flare guns when he ran out of those. "Lydia will be spearheading this operation, so check in with her frequently. Those without radios, use the flares if you find anything and someone with a radio will come find you. No more than an hour out, then head back in, regroup, warm up. We're going to be smart about this."

Lydia had shown up mere moments behind the Sheriff, a cadre of local women in tow. They'd quickly taken over the kitchen in both the bunkhouse and the main house and were busily distributing thermoses of coffee, hot chocolate and tea. Any warm liquid that they could get their hands on was fair game. Heck, Grady thought he'd even seen one lady heating up the half-bottle of Jack he'd had in the cabinet. He kind of envied whatever lucky bastard got *that* thermos.

"Grady."

Grady turned to find Thompson right behind. All around them, ATVs and snowmobiles were roaring to life and girths and hooves were being checked. A few of the pairs were already disappearing into the shadows at the edge of the lit yard.

Thompson's face was solemn as he handed Grady a radio. "You stick with Isaiah. I don't trust him to not go off half-cocked. I'd prefer to keep him out of this, but I know that's not possible."

Grady took the radio, clenching the device hard until the plastic edges dug into his hand, even through the thick fabric of his glove. "I'll watch him," he promised. "Just...we're gonna find Josh, right? He'll be okay?"

Dang. Grady's voice sounded far too pleading for his liking, but for once he didn't get a snapped comment from Thompson. In fact, the man looked downright sympathetic—an emotion Thompson had never once aimed Grady's way in all the years they'd known each other.

"You really care for that kid, don't you?"

"Yeah," Grady said hoarsely. "He's special. I don't think any of us would make it, if we lost him."

If something had happened to Josh, it would spell the end of the Branch faster than anything—at least the Branch as he knew it. His guys would be devastated. Grady doubted they would stay. And he *knew* Isaiah wouldn't. Hell, even Grady didn't know if he would be able to face this place day after day.

"We'll find him," Thompson said. "Now you two be careful."

Grady nodded his agreement. Isaiah waited impatiently a few feet away, already seated on one of their snowmobiles. Grady joined him, swinging his leg over the seat behind his man.

"Take it easy," he cautioned Isaiah. "We'll find him, but not if you do something stupid."

Isaiah nodded, but his eyes still held a wild look that Grady didn't like. He sighed, knowing there was little he could do about it.

The snowmobile roared to life and they headed out with gathering speed into the driving snow. It took mere minutes to leave the warm lights of the ranch far behind as the snowstorm swallowed them up, leaving the two of them cocooned in a muffled, isolated world of white.

* * * *

Josh shoved his hands deeper into his pockets, curling his fingers into the warmth of his gloves. Since the snow had started falling a bit ago, he actually felt warmer. Some of the biting wind had eased. It was still cold, though. Really cold.

Josh had been stupid and he knew it.

At first, he'd just been going to the barn. The horses were always happy to see him—they always made him feel better. But then he got to thinking that Isaiah would want to talk, and that would be the first place his big brother would look. So he'd just...started walking. It had been a dumb thing to do, really dumb.

Josh chewed on his lip, looking at the dark shapes of trees that surrounded him. He was lost. Completely and utterly. He'd started out following a small riding trail. That had turned into a deer path, then the falling snow had made even that vanish. Now he was stuck in the woods and he *knew* he wasn't far from the house. He just couldn't *find* it.

Josh took a few steps in one direction. Stopped. Looked around. He tried to remember all those survival tips Joseph had drilled into him. He was supposed to stay in one place but it was so cold. Josh didn't want to stop moving.

A dark smudge on the horizon caught his attention. It didn't look like a tree. It looked bigger. And square.

It was as good a goal as any, so Josh began slogging through the snow in that direction. At least there was one good thing about his situation—worrying about freezing to death was pushing all others issues aside for a while.

A branch smacked Josh in the face, snow spraying over his head and working its way under his hood. He shivered and shook, the instant chill seeping into his skin. He tripped on some unseen danger under a drift and dropped to his knees, ripping his hands from his pockets to catch his balance. He stayed like that for several minutes, breathing raggedly. He was starting to sweat from exertion. He thought that wasn't a good thing. At least, he seemed to recall a warning against overheating during a snowstorm. Probably one of those survival shows on the Discovery Channel. He maybe should have paid better attention, but he was more of a cartoon type.

Josh finally summoned the energy to push upright. Several large trees sheltered him, providing a bit of protection and blocking some of the wind and swirling snow.

And then he saw it. Just ahead, looming dark and cold and oh so welcoming. One of the line cabins.

Josh grabbed one of the trees, using it to steady himself as he took a few more steps forward. Then a few more.

Having a visible goal seemed to give him a burst of energy. He pushed through the drifts, some of them nearly waist-high. It seemed to take hours, but he was finally fumbling with the latch on the tiny cabin. He had to throw his whole body against the frozen wood, using his weight to shove it open. Rusted hinges squealed as the door gave way after several nerve-racking attempts.

Josh stumbled inside, shaking and whimpering. He shoved the door closed again, cutting the wind off abruptly. The sudden silence wasn't comforting, though. In fact, it was really rather eerie.

Josh just stood there, leaning against the door, trembling and panting. The inside of the cabin was dark, with only the barest hint of light seeping through the dusty windows. But it was enough to illuminate the small wood stove.

And the pile of wood next to it.

Josh weaved his way across the few feet and dropped to his knees in front of the cast iron stove. He had to pull his gloves off in order to pry the door open, frozen fingers clumsy on the catch.

Josh was going to give a big hug to whoever had used the cabin last. They'd left the stove primed and ready for use.

Now he just had to find some matches.

Chapter Twenty-One

The headlight on the snowmobile illuminated the path in front of them. The beam of light was dotted with the steady fall of snow. The wind whipped the snow into a frenzy and piled it up in heaps along fences and trees. That same wind cut through Grady's coat with terrifying ease. His chest, pressed up closely against Isaiah's back, was warm enough, as were the arms he had wrapped around Isaiah's bulky coat. His back, though, was freezing. He was half tempted to ask Isaiah to stop for a minute so he could turn around. Warm up the other side.

He bit his tongue, knowing that Isaiah wouldn't appreciate any attempt at levity at the moment. And it was for damn sure that he wouldn't stop. Not for Grady. Not for anything.

Except maybe for that tree.

The vehicle's treads slid in the snow, picking up speed even though Isaiah was desperately squeezing the brakes. Grady hung on and resisted the urge to close his eyes as they skidded sideways in a spray of snow.

The snowmobile came to rest nearly touching the fallen tree in their path. The engine cut out with shocking suddenness, leaving an eerie silence in its wake. Grady leaned his forehead against Isaiah's back, heart pounding in his throat.

"Damn," he breathed. "That was much too close."

Isaiah didn't reply.

"Isaiah?" Grady lifted his head. His lover—former lover—sat stiffly, gloved hands still wrapped around the handlebars. "Isaiah?"

When Grady called Isaiah's name a third time with no response, he swung one leg over the seat. His feet hit the ground, boots sinking deeply into the snow. Dang. There must be nearly six inches on the ground already. At this rate, they would have a foot of snow within the next hour. If it kept coming…

Grady firmly shoved Josh's smiling face from his mind. He couldn't think about that, not right then.

Grady rounded the vehicle and put one hand over Isaiah's. "Darlin'? You okay?"

Isaiah's head hung low, his breathing ragged. "I'm such an idiot," he mumbled.

"It's okay. I know you're scared. I am, too. But you can't think about that now. We'll find him."

"That's not what I meant!" Isaiah's head shot up.

Grady's grip tightened on his fingers when he got a good look at Isaiah's anguished expression.

"I nearly got us both killed!"

Grady's eyes nearly crossed in confusion. "It's dark. And we're blasting through a forest during a snowstorm. It happens."

"I was going too fast and being reckless and you damn well know it!"

Grady bit his lip. There wasn't much he could say to that. Isaiah was right. He'd been going at dangerous speeds, considering the conditions. Grady hadn't figured a warning would do much good, so he'd kept his mouth shut.

"Isaiah—"

"I almost got *you* killed." Isaiah finally prised his fingers loose, shaking off Grady's touch to cup his face with icy cloth. "I can't lose you, too."

"Okay, that's enough," Grady snapped, shoving Isaiah's hands away. He hated the mere thought that Isaiah was giving in to despair. Where the heck was his Isaiah's famed stubbornness now? "You haven't lost anyone, not Josh and most certainly not me. So get a grip, start this sucker up, and let's get back to searching."

"I—"

"Not now." Grady's words came out in a deep growl he hadn't even known he was capable of. He climbed back on and dug his fingers into Isaiah's sides.

"Drive," he ordered.

Isaiah hesitated for a minute, but just when Grady was getting ready to yell at him again, he moved. The engine broke the stillness of the snowy forest with the force of a chainsaw through virgin timber. Grady leaned his weight back as Isaiah turned the vehicle and they headed out again.

Their allotted hour came and went twice while they drove steadily, cutting a meticulous swathe through the snow. Bushes were now buried, tree trunks coated with ice. Several times they'd been forced to detour around drifts that were simply too large to plough through. Grady's nose was frozen and his eyelashes were coated with flakes, dotting his vision with white. He could only imagine that it was ten times worse for

Isaiah, who was driving straight into the wind far too often.

Grady leant forward, pressing his cracked lips next to Isaiah's hood. They were going to have to head in, or risk ending up frozen together on this damned vehicle until spring.

Grady stiffened. "You see that?" he demanded.

Isaiah immediately slowed. "See what?"

Grady squinted to his left, eyes fixed on the sky visible above the skeletal treetops. "There!" He grabbed Isaiah's shoulder, yanking him around. "Flare!"

"Oh, thank God." Isaiah cranked the snowmobile around and aimed it at the nearest tree line. A few minutes later they burst free of the forest and onto the narrow dirt track that led from the ranch up to one of the line cabins. Isaiah opened the throttle up as much as possible in the direction of home and they tore along the packed snow. Grady just hung on. Each breath was a struggle. The flare meant they had found Josh, but was he all right? Injured? Alive?

The last one caused far too much pain. Grady leaned his weight forward, urging the roaring vehicle between his legs to go faster, safety be damned.

He had never been so glad to see the lights of the ranch flicker over that last hill. Revving engines, horses whinnying, men and women shouting, it all blended into a cacophony that defeated the strange silence the snowstorm was working so hard to maintain. They flew over the last hill, careening down the final stretch of driveway and into a madhouse of activity.

Isaiah leapt from the vehicle without turning it off. He was already halfway to the house by the time the kill switch activated.

Grady was right on his heels, unwrapping layers as he went, heedless of the cold still biting through him. They pounded up the front steps.

The living room was packed with people. Anybody else wanting in would have to hang their heads through a window. And there, sitting in the middle of the chaos, neatly swathed hood to boots in a thick red blanket, was Josh. Grady had to stop—clinging to the doorframe as his knees gave way. He gasped for breath, relief so strong he could taste it.

Isaiah shoved through the room. When people saw who was coming, they parted as best as they could, even though it involved getting very up close and personal with their neighbours. Giving a wordless shout of joy, he hauled Josh into his arms. The hood of Josh's coat dropped to reveal damp blond hair. And that beautiful smile that had haunted Grady for the last several hours.

"They found him at the cabin up off Barrow's Trace. Seems like he got lost, but was lucky enough to stumble onto the old foreman's place. Even managed to get a fire going in that ancient wood stove up there, though it's a miracle that he didn't burn the whole building down."

"Thank you," Grady said hoarsely.

"Forget it," Thompson said bluntly.

Then Thompson did something astonishing. He reached out and clapped Grady on the shoulder. A brief squeeze followed before he cleared his throat.

At the sound, Josh looked over. He spotted Grady and thrust one arm out from his blanket. Grady's legs decided to work again and the next thing he knew, he was standing next to his entire world. He pulled them both close, a sob welling up as he buried his face against baby-soft hair and inhaled Josh's sweet scent.

"Thank God you're all right, kid," he whispered. "We were so scared."

Josh's fingers tapped a small rhythm on Grady's neck. "*Sorry.*"

"Doesn't matter," Grady said. "You're home and safe. Nothing else matters."

In that instant, with Isaiah's firm body pressed against his side and Josh snuggled between them once again, Grady came to a decision. Nothing was as important to him as these two people. Nothing. If the good people of Edmonton didn't like it, wouldn't let them live in peace, they'd go somewhere where they could. All three of them. As much as he loved this ranch, it wasn't enough anymore. Without Josh and Isaiah, it would just be an empty place full of memories and loss.

Grady could feel eyes boring into him, so many people staring at the two men embracing in their midst, but he didn't give a shit anymore. Let them look.

Thompson cleared his throat again. "All right, everyone, let's head out. It's gonna be hard enough getting back to town, no sense letting the snow pile up any more."

That got Grady's attention and he pulled back a bit until he could meet Thompson's eyes. "I can't thank everyone enough for helping search for him. Anyone who wants is welcome to stay here until the snow lets up. There's some empty rooms in the bunkhouse and I've got a couple of couches. Ya'll have risked more than enough for us tonight. I'd hate to see someone get hurt going home."

It was the least he could do. At heart, these were good people. They might not understand his sexual leanings—might, in fact, hate them—but when it had counted, they'd stepped up and offered their help with no thoughts for themselves, no nasty words or harsh expressions. He owed them a lot for that.

A few people accepted the offer. The Branch's guys had been huddled on the couch around Josh when Grady and Isaiah had arrived, and now they stood to get people settled down for the night. All three of them stopped to give Josh a quick squeeze or ruffle his hair. Tommy bent over to get a quick hug.

"Glad you're still in one piece, squirt. The big guys were 'bout ready to start opening up bears to find you."

"Now, Tommy," Grady teased. "You know there aren't any more bears in this part of Wyoming."

"Sure thing, boss," Tommy said with a wink. "Whatever helps you sleep at night."

Soft laughter followed Tommy as the room began to clear. Lydia came in with a couple of mugs of hot chocolate.

"Put that boy down before he dies of heat stroke," she scolded gently, her pale blue eyes bright. "Let's get him unwrapped and some food in him."

Josh giggled as Isaiah set him on his feet and began unwinding the blanket. Under that was another blanket. Then a coat. Then...

"Are you even in here?" Isaiah asked. Josh giggled louder.

"That's a lovely sound," Lydia declared. She beamed, her face radiating happiness. That was Lydia—she'd been a godsend to more than a few people over the years. What made her so popular, though, wasn't the fact that she was always cheerful, always looking for the bright side of any situation. No, it was the way she took genuine delight in the feelings of those around her. Lydia was now in her early fifties and unmarried but, as she always said, she was too busy taking care of the town to add a husband to the mix.

Between the three of them, they finally managed to free Josh from his cloth confinement.

"Lydia? We're heading home now." Eva Pritchard hovered in the doorway, face anxious, although she smiled at the sight of the happy little boy standing near the couch. "Would you like us to give you a ride?"

Eva and her husband had been one of the first couples to arrive when the call came out, despite the fact that she'd never made any secret of her hatred of 'that kind.' Heck, last time Grady had gone to town, the woman had crossed to the other side of the street to avoid coming near him. John Pritchard, on the other hand, wasn't the vocal sort. He let Eva do most of the talking. Whether her opinions were the same as his was anyone's guess.

"No, thank you, Eva. I believe I'll take the boys up on the offer to stay the night. I'll make a big breakfast for them in the morning and get someone to drive me home later."

"If you're sure." Eva's lips pressed together. She clearly wanted to argue, but no one argued with Lydia.

"I'm sure," Lydia replied firmly.

The front door closed after Eva a few minutes later.

"Why don't you and Josh go find something to eat?" Grady told Lydia. "I'm going to go out and thank everyone who's leaving, get them on their way. Isaiah, would you mind making up the guest bed for Lydia tonight?"

"Sure." Isaiah reached over and ran his hand through Josh's hair again, eyes soft. The man just couldn't seem to stop touching his younger brother, as if to assure himself that Josh was unharmed.

"Nonsense," Lydia declared. "You boys need to eat, too."

"Oh, we will," Grady said with a smile. "But later."

She shook her head and held out her hand. "Come on, Josh. We'll let them fool around while we get something warm in our tummies. I made chilli."

Josh hummed happily and took her hand, clearly willing to follow Lydia just about anywhere she led. Particularly if she led him to the kitchen and food.

Grady grabbed his coat again and prepared to head back outside. Isaiah stopped him with a light touch of his hand.

"Hey," he said. "It's okay now."

"I'm fine."

"Sure you are."

Before Grady could blink, he was held tightly in Isaiah's embrace. His wall broke and Grady let out a shaky breath, hands gripping Isaiah's shoulders tightly.

"Damn, I was so scared," he confessed.

"Me, too," Isaiah replied. He pressed a soft kiss to Grady's forehead. Grady relished the contact, feeling the promise of that kiss clear down to his still-numb toes. "Talk later?"

"Yeah." Grady brushed his lips with Isaiah's, their mouths sliding gently together before parting. "Be back soon."

Grady reluctantly went to the front door. He stopped just in front of the solid wood, took a deep breath and zipped up his coat, feeling something like a soldier donning his armour for battle. Now that the crisis was over...

He told himself to stop being such a coward and yanked open the door. No matter what reaction he got, Grady wasn't a complete boor. His mama had taught him manners, after all. When someone helped you out like the local people had tonight, you thanked them. A lot.

* * * *

Isaiah stuck his head around the open door of the guest room. "Got everything you need, Lydia?"

Lydia shooed him out with a scowl, though her eyes were bright and laughing. "I'm fine. Go to bed before you fall over."

"If you need anything at all—"

"Isaiah," she said firmly, in that authoritative way the woman had.

Isaiah chuckled and dipped his head, tipping an imaginary hat. "Yes, ma'am."

"Oh, Isaiah?"

Isaiah turned back around.

"Don't worry so much." Her lips curved up into a gentle smile, rife with understanding. "Everything will work out just fine."

"If you say so."

"I do, indeed."

"Goodnight, Lydia."

"Goodnight, dear."

Isaiah knew he should go to bed. He was tired and Grady was waiting for him, he had been for nearly a half hour. Isaiah just couldn't seem to settle. His nerves were all jittery. He forced his feet down the hall towards the room he and Grady had been sharing for the last...damn, had it only been two weeks? Things felt so right with Grady, so natural, it was as if they'd always been together.

Despite his resolve, Isaiah's feet slowed as he neared Josh's door, nearly closed but for a small crack that let a narrow band of light slip out onto the carpet. Isaiah reached out, before pulling his hand back. He couldn't resist, though. Palm flat on the wood, he pushed the door open gently. The curtains were drawn tightly against the faint moon, mostly to help block some of the chill that insisted on seeping through the window. Josh was one of those strange people who actually slept better with a bit of light in the room and, until it had turned so cold, Isaiah would often come in at night to find the curtains flung wide, moonbeams lighting the small space brightly. Tonight, Josh had to settle for the night light plugged in next to the bedroom door.

The light did help in one area. Isaiah was able to walk with quiet feet over to Josh's bed without tripping over the scattered items on the floor. Isaiah's lips tipped up. Past time for the kid to clean his room. Josh was a great kid, in general, but he wasn't perfect by any means. He avoided cleaning his room with the same dedication found among children the world over.

Isaiah stopped by the bed, studying the slumbering figure as he did many nights. He figured it was the one parenting thing he'd got in spades, this urge to check on the kid at night. Josh had kicked his comforter to one side again and Isaiah smiled as he tugged the covers back into place, pausing to lightly brush blond strands of hair off his familiar features. Josh looked so damn young when he slept. Well, he was young. Normally, though, his features were so full of energy and life, body in constant motion.

Without that, he appeared so much smaller and fragile.

"I could have lost you tonight," Isaiah whispered softly to the sleeping boy. His throat closed up and tears burned in his eyes. Isaiah wiped them away, not really caring that he was being so emotional. He figured he was entitled. In the past few months, Josh had become more than his brother, had become as good as his son. Any parent was excused from shedding a few – or even more than a few – tears at the near miss they'd had tonight.

Isaiah leaned over to brush one last kiss on Josh's forehead, tugged the already perfect covers up a little more firmly around thin shoulders, and finally made himself leave. He closed the door softly, leaving it cracked open a little bit, and rested his head against the wall for a second. *What are we –*

No, he wasn't going to do this right now. He was tired and wrung out and just wanted to climb into bed with his Grady. No more worrying tonight.

Isaiah knew that was far easier thought than accomplished, but he was damn well going to try.

Grady was just a huddled lump in the middle of the queen-sized bed when Isaiah stepped into the room. He stripped quickly, shivering in the chilly air, and eagerly climbed into bed. He yanked the covers up to nearly over his head and cuddled in close to the nice warm body already there.

"Hmmm. Where've you been?" Grady asked sleepily.

"Putting Josh to bed." Isaiah snagged Grady around the waist and pulled the man closer. He slid his cold feet between his lover's legs, chuckling a bit when Grady yelped.

"Damn, you're cold."

"It's still snowing."

"Marvellous." Grady turned his head into the pillow, already almost asleep again.

"I've been thinking—"

"Shh," Grady ordered. "Sleeping now. We can talk in the morning."

"I don't want to wait."

"Isaiah."

Isaiah sat up in bed and yanked the covers off Grady's head. He got a muffled curse as one big hand swatted at him.

"It's cold, Isaiah!"

What did Isaiah care? He hadn't warmed up yet. Yeah, he was exhausted, too. The tension and stress had played merry havoc with his muscles. His whole body felt heavy, worn out.

The rest of him, however, was wired up like he'd taken a straight IV of caffeine. He couldn't settle. Grady had wanted to talk earlier, so they were going to talk. Maybe then he'd be able to unwind enough to actually close his eyes.

"Grady."

Grady rolled over onto his back, flinging his arm over his eyes. "All right," he muttered. "You've now officially woken me up. So talk."

Isaiah drew absent circles on Grady's shoulder. "Do you think tonight might have changed some people's minds?"

Grady lifted his arm enough to peek at Isaiah through one narrowed eye. "Does it matter?"

"I guess not." Isaiah shrugged. "But we could have so easily lost Josh tonight. It kind of puts things in perspective."

Grady heaved a sigh, his arm dropping away entirely. Isaiah shoved himself up until he was sitting against the headboard, Grady's arm around his waist and idly stroking his opposite hip.

This. This was what Isaiah would miss the most, if he left Grady behind. Not the sex, though that was admittedly world-shaking at times. Not having someone there to watch Josh when Isaiah was frustrated and out of patience and just needed someone else to take over for a while. No, it was this casual affection he would miss, snuggling close to someone to exchange lazy words, without really caring what those words were. The small touches and the absent caresses that neither of them were even conscious of.

"You're right," Grady admitted. Isaiah jerked his head around, preoccupied enough that he had to scramble for a minute to remember what they were talking about.

"Nearly losing Josh…" Grady paused and licked his lips. "You're right. And my perspective has definitely changed. If you and Josh do decide to leave, you won't be going alone."

Isaiah stilled, heart pounding. Did that mean…*surely not*. "You would come with us?" he asked, barely daring to hope.

"Yeah, I would come with you."

"But the Branch, it's everything to you," Isaiah protested, mostly out of disbelief. The last thing he wanted to do was talk Grady out of this particular idea. But at the same time, he didn't want Grady to lose such a vital part of himself. He had a mental image of Grady, pale and worn, lost without the place that was buried so deeply within his blood.

"No," Grady corrected. "It *was* everything to me. I've found something better."

Isaiah pounced, lips crashing against Grady's in a violent kiss as he tried to express the emotions that he didn't have the words for. Grady pulled him closer and returned the embrace clash for clash, lips nipping and tugging, eating at each other with such force that Isaiah tasted a hint of blood.

"You'd really do that for us?" Isaiah finally had to pull back to breathe. His chest rose and fell rapidly as he struggled to get his body and emotions under control. Grady's face was flushed, cock pressing insistently into Isaiah's leg through the covers. Isaiah had never seen his hazel eyes so deep and dark.

Grady shook his head. "No, I'd do it for me."

"Thank you," Isaiah whispered.

"But..."

Isaiah squeezed his eyes shut. Oh, damn. Here it came.

"But I think we're giving up too soon."

His eyes shot back open. Grady studied him with serious eyes. The man even licked his lips a touch nervously.

"I won't risk —"

"I don't think it will come to that," Grady interrupted. "I really don't. Besides, what we have here, isn't it worth fighting for?"

Isaiah sighed and dropped forward onto his lover's chest, arousal fading into a swamp of utter exhaustion. He was just so tired. Tired of the mental tug-of-war, tired of obsessing over that damn letter, just plain tired.

Grady seemed to understand. He tangled his hand in Isaiah's hair, tugging until Isaiah looked up from his sprawled — and very comfortable — position.

"This is why I wanted to wait until tomorrow to talk," he chided gently. "Neither one of us is in any kind of shape to be making important decisions right now. Just know whatever we decide to do, we do it together."

"Thank you," Isaiah whispered. He dropped his head back onto Grady's chest, pressing a soft kiss to the closest nipple. Grady groaned.

"Darlin', as much as I love your mouth on me, I don't think I'm up for it."

"You were a minute ago," Isaiah teased.

"Yeah, but that was a minute ago."

Grady slid down on the mattress, pulling Isaiah with him. He wrapped the covers more firmly around both of them. Their legs and arms tangled together, bodies curled into each other.

"Sleep," Grady ordered. "We'll talk more in the morning, when we're both more coherent."

"Yes, boss."

"Jerk."

"Doofus."

"I—"

"Go to sleep, Isaiah."

"'M not Josh."

"I know."

"'Kay."

Isaiah quickly lost the battle with Morpheus, eyes sliding shut on the sight of Grady's affectionate gaze.

Chapter Twenty-Two

Isaiah let the front door slam behind him, pausing briefly to knock a bit of snow off his boots. The weather had eased, warming up and providing them with a bit of a lull in the snow. Blinding sun aside, it still took a blasted long time for four feet of snow to melt.

"Dillon!" he shouted. "You in here?"

His voice echoed along the hallways and Isaiah sighed. He was just about to turn around and head back outside when he heard a loud thud, followed by a curse.

Grady came thumping down the stairs, grumpy-faced and coated in dust.

"What the hell have you been doing?" Isaiah asked with amusement.

"I was looking for something in the attic."

Isaiah grinned. "You've got cobwebs in your hair. Maybe I should check you for spiders."

Grady scowled. "Did you want something in particular, or just to pester me?"

Isaiah waved the folder in his hand. "Just got done meeting with Edwards."

Grady's grumpiness vanished under anxiety. "What did he say? Is everything okay?"

It had only been a few weeks since they almost lost Josh, but the situation had most definitely improved. Isaiah had promptly hired a lawyer, who had sent out a lot of letters that Isaiah couldn't understand. Josh running away, too, must have got through to the sheriff. Oh, he was still an ass, but Isaiah kind of figured it was simply the man's natural personality. In any case, ever since that horrible night, he'd stopped harassing them or making threats. The sheriff must have worked on the mayor, too. They'd never apologised, never come right out and said 'we're leaving you alone now', but no one had ever followed up on the letter, either. Isaiah figured they were safe.

Either that or some lawyer-type had pounded some sense into the town officials' heads. Without panic clouding his view, Isaiah had been able to do what he should have done in the first place—dig for information. He'd talked to people in social services, child advocates, lawyers...anyone he could find.

The news had been liberating. While Social Services could often be pesky about gay couples, he was family, which seemed to make all the difference. Just to be on the safe side, though, Isaiah was working on adoption proceedings. He was still trying to talk Grady into doing the same. If anything happened to Isaiah, he wanted Josh staying here.

"All signed, sealed, and delivered," Isaiah announced. "Josh is officially and legally mine and the good town leaders can go jump in the creek."

"Thank God," Grady breathed.

The man looked so relieved and happy that Isaiah simply had to take a kiss. One kiss turned into two. Then three. Isaiah pushed back, panting and hard and really wishing they had time to take this upstairs. Hell, the couch would do.

"Babe, we have to go," Isaiah said reluctantly, running his palms along Grady's shoulders. "Josh will be waiting."

"I guess."

Isaiah gave him another kiss, making sure to keep this one to a quick peck. "Grab the rest of your gear. We've got reservations, huh?"

They were going on vacation. One whole weekend in Denver. Isaiah couldn't wait. They were picking Josh up from school and dropping him off at Emily's on the way. Emily was the unofficial Barton ASL expert. She and Josh had bonded right away and she was more than willing to watch him for a couple of days.

Josh was safe and a permanent part of their lives. Grady only freaked out about their relationship once a week now. The boys had all been given raises. They were in the process of expanding the breeding barns and planning to spend more time focused on breeding horses in the spring — Grady hoped to eventually phase out the cattle entirely, although Isaiah wasn't so sure that was the best idea. And now they were on their way to take a well-deserved few days off playing around in Denver.

Yeah, life was looking pretty good.

Isaiah smacked Grady on the butt. "Move it, cowboy," he teased.

Grady growled, but went.

Isaiah double-checked that everything had been packed. The extended cab of his truck was crammed full. Grady came out with two more bags and Isaiah groaned.

"Babe, what the hell do you need all that crap for? I don't think we've got room."

"It'll fit," Grady replied with a stubborn expression. Isaiah stepped back and waved his hand.

"Go for it," he stated, then watched with amusement as Grady stuffed and shoved and finally managed to wedge his bags into a teeny open space.

They climbed in and headed out with one last honk and wave at the distant bulky shadow that could only be Tommy.

The drive flashed by, familiar enough that Isaiah could zone out a bit. Not much traffic, and the roads were finally clear of snow.

The long, low building of Barton's grade school loomed ahead and Isaiah pulled in, parking in front of the kerb. He shut the truck off and stepped out, shoving his sunglasses on top of his head and squinting at the flare of sunlight that hit his eyes. On the other side of the truck, Grady leaned against the open door, waiting patiently.

A bell rang in the distance and Isaiah winced. Here it came.

Children began pouring out of the building, loud and skittering. It reminded Isaiah a bit of a swarm of locusts. God, it was a frightening sight.

"Gonna run, darlin'?" Grady drawled.

"You'd be right behind me, babe," Isaiah retorted.

"Damn straight."

Isaiah chuckled, scanning the mass of little people for one familiar blond head. He didn't see it, but that was okay. He was safe on the far side of the truck, well protected from the invasion.

A small tyke about two-foot-nothing tripped and slid to the concrete, wails filling the air. Grady was over there in a second, big body crouched down as he soothed the boy. Isaiah shook his head. That was Grady. Softest heart in the West.

"Doesn't look too bad," Grady said, brushing dirt off the offered palms. "Hush, now, Barry-boy. I think I see your mama comin', so wipe those tears, huh?"

The little one sniffed a couple of times, nodded, and let Grady help him up.

"Barry, did you trip again?" Melinda Pierce shook her head, ruffling the dark hair. "I swear, boy, we're gonna get you some tighter shoes."

She turned to Grady with a bright smile. "You do have a way with children," she complimented.

Isaiah straightened with a jerk. Well, damn it all, she was making a move on his man.

Grady gave one of his bright smiles — as normal, completely oblivious to the come-on. And for the love of heaven, a woman with a five-year-old should *not* look so lecherous.

"Kids and animals," Grady agreed. "But then, they're easy, aren't they? Just love 'em."

"Such a nice sentiment," she murmured, glancing up coyly.

Isaiah rolled his eyes and stepped away from the truck. For Grady, he'd brave the mob of pint-sized humans. It was quite the sacrifice. He hoped Grady appreciated it.

"Grady! Isaiah!"

Isaiah's attention was diverted when he heard Tony call his name. The school principal came jogging down the front steps of the school, seemingly oblivious to the screaming hordes darting around his knees.

The skinny man came to a halt near Grady, nearly bouncing in place. Oh, to have that kind of energy. Then again, the man probably needed it. He was, after all, a grade school principal. *There's a special place in heaven reserved for those brave souls*, Isaiah thought. He certainly didn't envy the man.

"Hey, Tony," Isaiah called. He nodded politely to Melinda, who gathered up little Barry and left. Not without a few backward glances, however, and a wistful twist of her lips as her father-seeking attempts were thwarted once again. Isaiah was getting damn good at it. It was amazing. Grady might not be all that popular over in Edmonton—although it was getting better—but the good single mothers of Barton came after him in swarms.

"I was hoping I could catch you two before you left," Tony said, grinning widely. "Emily tell you yet?"

"Tell us what?" Grady asked.

"Well, I've managed to talk her into coming to the school one day a week and teaching a class on ASL. She's also willing to do an adult night class for anyone who's interested. I thought I'd try and convince you guys to help."

"I'm sure we could work out something," Isaiah agreed.

"It's great of her to do that," Grady added. "And you, too. The school board went for it? I mean, Josh is just one kid."

"Ah, but I'm very persuasive." Tony waggled his eyebrows and Isaiah smothered a snort. "Besides, I think it's a fantastic opportunity for these kids. We already teach them Spanish, why not sign language? It'll be good for the kids to learn, plus we can work in some fantastic lessons about disabilities at the same time. Tolerance and diversity, yeah?"

"Wish you could teach a few people in Edmonton those lessons," Isaiah muttered.

Tony winced. "Yeah, sorry. How is everything on the home front?"

"Could be better, could be worse. There are certain businesses that won't let us through the door, but it appears that the mayor has backed off on the custody thing for now."

"Well, that's a relief," Tony declared. "Because that was just stupid. As for the businesses — who needs them? I'd rather take my patronage elsewhere, anyway."

"Same here."

Grady pretended to watch the front doors for Josh, his silence making Isaiah grimace. Six weeks and the man was still struggling to adjust. Still tended to blame himself for any harsh words aimed their way over their sexual preference. Isaiah was working on helping him, but it was hard for someone to change the habits of a lifetime. At least Grady had avoided any fights recently. Of course, that might be because they never let him venture into Edmonton alone. Hey, Isaiah was willing to play dirty when it came to the safety of his man.

Tony said a cheerful goodbye, scampering off to answer another parent's summons. The mass of children was thinning out, buses pulling away from the kerb with squealing tires and the hiss of closing doors.

Isaiah slung an arm over Grady's shoulder and gave his partner a quick squeeze, easily ignoring the way the broad shoulders tensed under his touch.

"Looking forward to a few days off?" he asked.

"Hmmm," Grady hummed in agreement. Isaiah almost whooped in triumph when Grady leaned into him, just the tiniest bit. Every step forward was counted as a victory in this battle.

"Finally." Isaiah stepped away, waving at the bundle of energy hopping down the stairs. "Where have you been?" Isaiah asked, taking Josh's Transformers backpack. God, it weighed a ton. What were the teachers trying to do, give kids back problems before they even hit puberty?

Josh smirked and shook his head, one finger pressing against his lips.

"A surprise, huh?" Grady drawled. He pulled off his hat and dropped it on Josh's head. Isaiah smiled at the way the brim slipped down over Josh's eyes.

The kid pushed it back, grinning up at them.

"Let me guess," Isaiah replied dryly. "It has something to do with an upcoming school event."

"And what do you want to bet that you've been volunteered?" Grady teased.

"God." Isaiah shuddered dramatically, earning a light giggle from Josh. "Get in the truck, you two," he scolded playfully. "We've got plans."

Josh pumped one fist in the air and climbed into the truck, Grady's hand on his butt helping him up. Short legs and raised pickup cabs didn't mix.

Isaiah stowed Josh's backpack and rounded the truck. He fired up the engine and smiled, listening to the soft sounds of laughter as he pulled away.

Yeah, life was looking pretty good, indeed.

Epilogue

Darn, irritating...

Isaiah flung his arm out, slapping blindly at the table. After a minute of searching, he finally found the snooze button. He rolled over, folding the pillow over his head.

The buzzing continued. He groaned, pulling the pillow tighter around his ears. When that didn't work, he hit the button a few more times.

After several sluggish moments, realisation crept into his fuzzy brain. Not the alarm clock.

"Hellfire and damnation," he cursed. As usual, the sheets had inexplicably wrapped themselves around his legs. He struggled to free himself as the blasted phone continued to ring.

Isaiah squinted at the glowing green numbers of his alarm clock. *Oh.* It wasn't that late, so it hopefully wasn't someone calling about a dire emergency. Of course, now he was up, so he might as well answer the darned thing.

Isaiah managed to escape from the sheets. He staggered across the room, groaning as his thighs protested. *Stupid stepladder, and then the garland.* His ears were still ringing from childish squeals and if he never tasted mulled cider again it would be too soon.

He dug through the pockets of his inexplicably glitter-coated jeans, crowing triumphantly when his fingers closed around the hard plastic case.

"'Lo?"

"Finally."

A wide smile spilled across Isaiah's face. He flopped back onto the bed, grinning like an idiot. "Hey, you."

"I didn't wake you, did I?" Grady asked with a light teasing note in his voice.

"You did, actually." Isaiah made the admission without the slightest bit of shame. He'd had a rough day. He was entitled to crash early.

Grady's warm laugh came through the phone. Isaiah never got tired of the sound. "It's only...what, nine-thirty there?"

"You try spending an entire day surrounded by wild creatures hyped up on sugar cookies. See how you feel."

"Ah, I almost forgot. How did the decorating go?"

"Slowly," Isaiah said wryly. "You gonna be back in time?"

"You know it."

Isaiah hummed in contentment. Despite the nagging headache and the sore back, he was completely and utterly happy. Of course, he'd be happier if a certain someone was in bed with him instead of halfway across the country.

"I miss you," Isaiah murmured.

"Miss you, too."

"Everything going okay out there?"

"Fantastic. We're looking pretty good for making the final cut."

"That's great!" Isaiah sat up, loving the sound of excitement in his Grady's voice. The Shires had taken everyone by surprise. Their first little foal was sweeping up awards at shows region-wide. Grady had finally taken a chance and hauled Gypsum out to California for a show, where the prize money — and the accolades — were a bit bigger. He'd been reluctant. Christmas was right around the corner and it would just about kill Grady if he couldn't be there.

Hence the day spent atop a stepladder. With Grady gone for nearly a week, Isaiah had been at loose ends. It made him do stupid things. Like volunteer to help with Josh's school Christmas party. Setup and all.

"Hey, did I lose you there?" Grady's voice was soft and the affection — plain even at a distance — eased Isaiah's stress, his headache melting away.

"No, still here. Just thinking."

"Good thoughts, I hope."

"Oh, yeah. Very good." Isaiah made sure to add a little tease to the words, knowing he'd succeeded when a low groan caressed his ear.

"You're a wicked, wicked man," Grady scolded.

"But I'm *your* wicked man."

"That you are."

The loose board in the hallway squeaked loudly and Isaiah chuckled. "Sounds like someone is trying to sneak out to the barn again."

"Better go catch the squirt before he gets pneumonia. It's too damn cold for him to be sleeping in the stable."

"Yeah." Isaiah paused, reluctant to hang up. But the duties of parenthood called, so he just said, "Be safe and come home soon."

"Absolutely. Love you."

"Love you, too."

Isaiah hung up and reached for a pair of sweat pants, still smiling. Yeah, life had changed a lot since that phone call over a year ago. But maybe his life had needed a little bit of shaking up. Now? He wouldn't change a thing.

"Josh!" he yelled down the stairs, pulling his sweatshirt over his head. "Get your butt back up here!"

Nope. Not a darn thing.

About the Author

Born and raised in the middle of the Midwest, I have always been a dreamer. More often than not I could be found with my nose buried in a book (many of which I had to sneak past my parents). It wasn't long before I started trying my hand at writing more of the stories I loved. After years of penning tales that rarely left the hard drive of my computer, I discovered M/M romance. As with all genres, it wasn't long before my own characters started to take shape.

There is little I love more than wandering new places and, on occasion, entirely new worlds with my characters. They can range from cowboys to Victorian noblemen, accountants to shapeshifters, and everything in between. I write mainly m/m romance, usually with paranormal or fantasy elements. I willingly follow my characters wherever they decide to go, sometimes with unusual results. I have little control over their actions – any naughty behaviour is all their doing!

KM Mahoney loves to hear from readers. You can find her contact information, website details and author profile page at http://www.total-e-bound.com.

Total-E-Bound Publishing

www.total-e-bound.com

Take a look at our exciting range of literagasmic™
erotic romance titles and discover pure quality
at Total-E-Bound.

www.ingramcontent.com/pod-product-compliance
Lightning Source LLC
Chambersburg PA
CBHW030140180626
46812CB00002B/780